SITUATION: OUT OF CONTROL
DEBRA WEBB

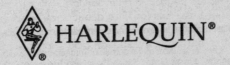

HARLEQUIN®

TORONTO • NEW YORK • LONDON
AMSTERDAM • PARIS • SYDNEY • HAMBURG
STOCKHOLM • ATHENS • TOKYO • MILAN • MADRID
PRAGUE • WARSAW • BUDAPEST • AUCKLAND

ISBN 0-373-22801-5

SITUATION: OUT OF CONTROL

Printed in U.S.A.

ABOUT THE AUTHOR

Debra Webb was born in Scottsboro, Alabama, to parents who taught her that anything is possible if you want it badly enough. When her husband joined the military, they moved to Berlin, Germany, and Debra became a secretary in the commanding general's office. By 1985 they were back in the States, and with the support of her husband and two beautiful daughters, Debra took up writing full-time and in 1998 her dream of writing for Harlequin came true. You can write to Debra with your comments at P.O. Box 64, Huntland, Tennessee 37345 or visit her Web site at www.debrawebb.com to find out exciting news about her next book.

Books by Debra Webb

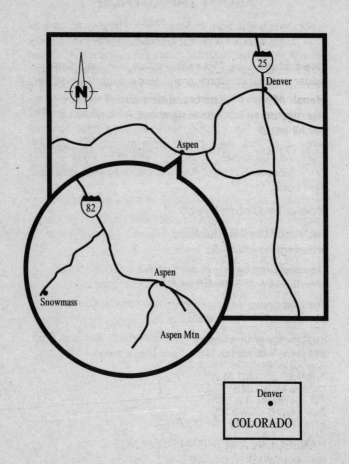

CAST OF CHARACTERS

Jayne Stephens—Mountain rescue assistant team leader and backcountry travel guide. Faithful daughter.

Heath Murphy—The brand-new Colby Agency investigator on his first assignment. A man with a painful past.

Cole Danes—Internal Affairs investigator assigned to ferret out the leak at the Colby Agency. A man with secrets of his own.

Victoria Colby-Camp—Head of the Colby Agency.

Lucas Camp—Deputy director of Mission Recovery and Victoria's loving husband. He will do anything to protect the woman he loves.

Howard Stephens—A man with a connection to Errol Leberman. The father that Jayne trusts.

Walt Messina—Mountain rescue team leader and the owner of Happy Trails Tours.

Rafe Gonzales—Owner of the Altitude Bar and Grill and Jayne's landlord. He is very protective of his one tenant.

First I'd like to take this opportunity to say a special thanks to all the wonderful folks at eHarlequin.com. You provide authors and readers alike with a home away from home, a wonderful place to chat and meet new friends. And to read great stories! Thanks for all you do!

This book is dedicated to a handsome young man who I know has a bright future ahead of him. He's not only good-looking, but he's intelligent and loyal—the best traits a man can possess. This one is for you, Chad, a terrific nephew! Love, Aunt Deb.

Chapter One

Victoria Colby-Camp stared out the window of her new home, watching the scene that would have once torn at her heart with an unbearable ruthlessness. Children, backpacks swinging, rushed to climb into minivans and SUVs. Harried mothers slid behind steering wheels all the while calling off the usual morning checklist. "Buckle up!" "Do you have your lunch?" "Where's your coat?"

Victoria had missed out on most of those tender years with her son. She'd scarcely gotten him through first grade before evil had descended upon her family.

She drew in a deep breath and pushed away the pain that lingered still. It was over now. Her son was home and safe from the bastard who had tortured him. Jim Colby was healed, for the most part. However, there were changes not so easily overcome. The brainwashing techniques that had been used on her son had lingering effects. But he was strong. Just like his father had been. He would continue to improve, continue to regain the life that had been stolen from him. And, most important, he had a woman who loved him close at his side.

Victoria smiled. Another woman besides his mother. Tasha North had proven a vital element in his recovery. Victoria thanked God for her each and every day. Jim and Tasha were currently spending a much-needed getaway in the Caribbean. The doctors had agreed to a two-week hiatus from treatment after three long months of intensive therapy. Though Victoria missed him immensely, she knew that her son was in capable hands with Tasha.

The smile faded from Victoria's lips. Despite the joy of having her son back and knowing that Leberman was rotting in hell, there were still questions related to his legacy of terror. Questions that had to be answered, though she was loath to admit as much.

Lucas was right. They had to discover how Leberman had gotten his information and they had to find the man who had helped him kidnap Jim all those years ago. He would have answers they desperately needed.

Victoria would never believe that a member of her own staff had knowingly betrayed her. Never. Nothing anyone could say would convince her. However, she did recognize that there were ways of getting information without a person's knowledge. Even her seemingly invincible Colby agents were human. That, in her opinion, was the only way the information Leberman used could have come from her agency.

With that solemn realization, she had reluctantly agreed to Lucas's plan. An internal affairs investigation would launch today. She swallowed, a knot of emotion making the task near impossible. No matter how much sense this step made, no matter how good the man in charge of the investigation, Victoria couldn't help feeling guilty.

She felt like a Judas.

Everyone at the agency insisted that they understood and welcomed the scrutiny. And yet, it felt utterly wrong. But it was the only way. She could not accept the risk that the second man involved with Leberman's long-ago plot to destroy the Colbys might learn of some future tactic that involved Jim. The doctors had repeatedly acknowledged that some parts of Jim's memory could not be unlocked.

As a longtime secret agent for the United States government, Lucas knew far too much about mind control techniques to assume that the inaccessible parts of Jim's memory were harmless. It would be just like Leberman to have built in an encore—a backup plan in case his machinations failed. All it would take was the right word or set of circumstances and a deeply embedded neuro-command might just overtake Jim's ability to think for himself. Might force him to do the unthinkable.

That possibility represented a risk Victoria would not take.

She had to trust Lucas as well as the man he'd chosen to oversee this investigation. Someone outside the Colby Agency. Someone who would be completely objective.

Cole Danes.

Victoria had only met him once, but she had immediately sensed a coldness about him. He appeared distant and untouchable, unfeeling actually. His reputation marked him as relentless, savagely so.

But Lucas trusted him.

She had to remind herself of that all-important fact.

She glanced at the clock on the mantel—8:00 a.m. The meeting would start now…and she couldn't be there. Lucas had given her orders to stay clear of the investigation. Any interference on her part would be detrimental and only prolong the discomfort.

This had to be done.

She understood that.

But she didn't have to like it.

"I've prepared your favorite breakfast," Lucas said as he came up behind her.

She hadn't heard him come into the room. How long had he been watching? Unguarded, her every thought had certainly etched the echoing emotion on her face. He would have easily read each one. He knew her so very well.

Her husband slid his strong arms around her waist and pulled her against his reassuringly strong body. She felt the steady beat of his heart, experienced an instant sense of relief. "You have my word," he whispered softly against the shell of her ear, "that all will be well."

Tears brimmed before she could suppress another abrupt surge of emotion. How she prayed he was right. She gave herself a mental shake. How could she doubt

Lucas? He had never failed her. She leaned her head against his shoulder. "I know."

"This will be over very soon."

She nodded. Cole Danes had assured her that he would waste no time. He knew what to do and he would do it without hesitation or question. He was the best. His reputation unparalleled in the arena of internal affairs.

Still, the worry gnawing at her would not be allayed. Victoria placed her hand over Lucas's and said out loud the words that filled her heart with tormenting dread. "But nothing will ever be the same."

Lucas didn't have to say anything. He knew, just as she did, that this step would forever change the dynamics of the Colby Agency. There was no way to pretend away the inevitable.

Nothing would ever be the same.

Chapter Two

Inside the Colby Agency

Heath Murphy surveyed the conference room as the remainder of his colleagues at the Colby Agency made their way to fill the vacant seats around the long mahogany table. He nodded a greeting to Ric Martinez, the guy who'd taken Heath under his wing the past couple of months to show him the ropes. Ric and his lovely wife, Piper, had acquainted him with Chicago's nightlife and cultural offerings, as well, since Heath was new to the city in addition to being new at the agency.

More greetings were exchanged and coffee cups filled before the room settled, leaving the quiet crammed with simmering anticipation. Heath recognized all the faces, had been befriended by most. There were a couple folks from research who kept to themselves, offering only a cursory acknowledgement of other humans when absolutely necessary. Heath imagined that those guys spent so much time in cyberspace that they'd forgotten how to be truly social with like life forms.

Maxwell Pierce, Ethan Delaney, Nicole Reed-Michaels and Mildred Parker, just to name a few others, were the ones who went above and beyond the call to make the new feel welcome on a daily basis. Heath gave one person in particular an extra wide smile. Mildred, the secretary/personal assistant to the head of the agency. She kept everyone straight. Knew the Colby Agency inside out. He doubted there was a person here who could do without Mildred's special brand of guidance from time to time, especially a newbie like him.

The door closed and Heath glanced in that direction. Simon Ruhl and Ian Michaels, both second in command only to Victoria Colby-Camp herself, moved to the front of the room. Neither man looked particularly happy this Monday morning. Heath couldn't actually blame them. Like everyone else at the agency he'd been briefed on what was about to take place. And, like the rest, he felt somewhat less than comfortable with the situation though he didn't have a real problem with the process.

As a former police officer he was aware of what an internal affairs investigation involved. Depending on the investigator in charge it could get pretty ugly. But then, this wasn't an official police proceeding, this was a civilian firm. He doubted the inquiry would be anything like the real thing. He surveyed the polished, professional group seated around the table. He couldn't see these people tolerating the kind of crap cops had no choice but to endure. Heath clenched his jaw hard and forced the bitter memories away. He'd been cleared, eventually. No point going back down that road again. He wasn't a cop anymore. He was a private investigator. At one of the most prestigious firms in the country.

He didn't have to rehash the past.

He would not.

This was his home now.

Forcing himself to relax once more, he tuned out the past and focused on the pep talk Simon Ruhl had launched.

"We've all been briefed on the necessity of this investigation," Simon said. "I've been assured that it will be accomplished in as efficient and nondisruptive a manner as possible. However—" his gaze moved from face to face before he continued "—Ian and I will be available for anyone who wishes to talk or who has a problem with any part of the proceedings." He looked from one attentive listener to the next. "Do not hesitate to come forward at any time."

Acknowledging nods jogged through the group. Simon's words had the intended effect. Heath could feel the change in the atmosphere of the room already. Tension relented and anticipation receded to a degree. There was no reason to be concerned, that was the message Simon wanted to impress. No one present really believed that a traitor existed among their ranks.

Heath was too new to speculate but his gut feeling was that the internal affairs investigation would be an exercise in futility, not to mention a monumental waste of time. These were the good guys. He'd worked with enough bad guys to know the difference.

"From this moment forward and until this investigation is completed," Ian Michaels said, taking the floor, "you will take your instructions from Mr. Danes."

A new kind of hush fell over the room. Heath frowned. The apprehension ratcheted back up a few notches. Maybe the staff wasn't as prepared as he'd presumed. A ping of dread made his own instincts flinch, but he quickly dismissed the uneasiness. Semantics, method of delivery, those were the reasons for the sudden reversal in the climate of the room. From his observations Heath had noted one distinct difference between Simon Ruhl and Ian Michaels. Simon went the extra distance to smooth ruffled feathers, to inject calm. In vivid contrast, Ian's demeanor was distant, quietly intimidating. The man did not mince words. Yet he was well liked. Two very different men, both very good at their work. Like everyone else employed by this agency. Heath couldn't help feeling a little rush of pride at having been brought on board. This was his new home. He liked it and intended to make a fresh start here.

No looking back.

"And just when are we going to meet this Mr. Danes?" Mildred piped up with her usual blunt flair. Heath smiled. She was a definite original. One of a kind.

"Now is as good a time as any."

Every head in the room turned to stare in the direction of the unfamiliar voice. A stranger leaned casually against the wall next to the door. Heath felt certain he wasn't the only one who had not heard the newest arrival enter the conference room. As the man pushed off the wall and strolled leisurely to the front of the room, a different level of uneasiness nudged at Heath. Just who the hell was this guy? Anyone who could catch a room full of highly trained agents off guard was good.

Damn good.

Heath's gaze settled on the man in question as he assumed the position of authority as smoothly as drawing a breath. Simon and Ian stepped aside, giving him the floor without further ado. Ian settled into a chair next to his wife, Nicole, and Simon took the last remaining seat on the opposite end of the table. The whole transition of power took a single second with no pomp and circumstance.

The man at the front of the room braced his hands behind his back, assuming a typical military stance of attention. But there was nothing typical about his expression. He surveyed those seated around the table with a kind of primal intensity that spoke of extreme confidence and uncanny perception. This man would not only be very good at his work, he would also enjoy every moment of the effort as well.

Heath would bet almost anything that Mr. Cole Danes was not only ex-military, but ex-CIA, too. Or perhaps some group more subversive. Heath had met his kind before. Nothing would get in the way of the job. Ruthless was the word that came to mind.

Cole Danes trusted no one. Heath sensed with wrenching certainty that ice likely filled his veins. The man epitomized the phrase "commanding presence."

Tall; broad-shouldered; deep, authoritative voice. Total control. He would accept nothing less. His tailored suit, while elegant, suggested careful attention to detail. All business. But his overlong hair gave him the untrustworthy look of a shady character from the wrong side of the tracks and the silver hoop that winked from one ear only strengthened that perception. A dichotomy.

"My name is Cole Danes."

Heath's attention shifted forward once more. Now the games would begin.

"As Simon told you, I will conduct this investigation as quickly and with as little disruption to the status quo as possible. Each of you will be subjected to close scrutiny that will involve extensive background investigation and repeated interviews."

A tiny smile tugged at one corner of Heath's mouth. He didn't see the big deal in that. Hell, he'd been through that already just to be considered as a Colby Agency investigator.

"You may believe that you've been exposed to this very sort of investigation before." Danes's gaze settled on Heath as if he'd spoken his thoughts aloud. "Perhaps when you were hired."

Heath felt the hairs on the back of his neck stand on end. What was this guy? Psychic?

"Let me warn you now," Danes went on, his penetrating attention, thankfully, advancing to someone else, "this will be a new experience. That I can assure you. When I'm finished—" that relentless gaze moved from face to face while the room held its collective breath

"—I will know more about you than you know about yourself."

"That sounds strangely like a threat, Mr. Danes," Ian Michaels suggested in that quietly intimidating tone that marked him as a man who refused to be disconcerted by mere talk.

Danes relaxed his stance ever so slightly. His mouth quirked into a casual smile but there was no sign of amusement in his expression. "No, Mr. Michaels, that was not a threat at all." The smile vanished, ferocity lit in his eyes. "It was a promise." He turned back to the room at large. "Any questions?"

HEATH DIDN'T HANG around in the conference room when the briefing was over. He went to his office and closed the door, as did most everyone else. No one wanted to linger and risk being the first to be sacrificed on the Cole Danes altar of supremacy. Though Heath had only been at the agency a couple of months, he felt certain that no one had ever seen Ian Michaels and Simon Ruhl as furious as they were by Danes's cocky answer to Ian's question. Danes clearly didn't give a damn. He had his job to do and wasn't about to play nice.

Heath pushed aside the whole subject and directed his attention to reading reports. Simon had suggested that he read the past year's case reports in order to get a better handle on how the Colby Agency conducted business and the level of insight expected from him. He'd already worked on a couple of cases with other investigators. Soon he would get his first assignment. He wanted to be prepared. The internal affairs investigation notwithstanding, he really liked it here. He wanted to fit in and do a good job. It had been a while since he'd felt right with his life, professionally or personally.

Despite this morning's overbearing announcement by Danes, Heath wasn't worried. Cole Danes was looking for someone who'd fed information to Victoria's longtime enemy over a period of years. The guy, Leberman, had been eliminated before Heath received news he'd been hired. He had nothing to worry about in this investigation. Still, Danes made him uncomfortable.

Someone very much like Cole Danes had ended Heath's career as a cop. Well, that wasn't exactly true. Heath had been the one to resign on his own. But it was the kind of cold intimidation tactics he saw in Danes that had made him walk away. The distrust and suspicion heaped upon him had been a rude awakening for a guy who'd put in eight good years. Had never once gotten out of line or failed to do his duty.

In the end that hadn't counted for squat. He'd been looked upon as just as guilty as his partner until Heath had been cleared. What happened to innocent until proven guilty? Apparently during an internal affairs investigation there were no innocents. That was the part that bothered Heath the most. He'd trusted his partner and look where that had gotten him. Maybe Cole Danes wasn't so far off the mark. When things got down to the nitty-gritty a guy could only trust himself.

A cold hard fist of memory hit him square in the gut.

And then there were those times when he couldn't even trust himself.

A quick rap on his door jerked Heath from the troubling thoughts just as it opened.

"I need a few moments of your time, Mr. Murphy."

Cole Danes entered Heath's office and sat down before he could assimilate an appropriate response. Damn. Maybe this guy could read minds and wanted to make sure Heath didn't feel left out.

Heath set aside the report he'd been reading. Might as well get this over with. "What can I do for you, Mr. Danes?"

Piercing blue eyes studied him for what felt like a mini-eternity before an answer was forthcoming. "I'm aware that you've gone through an investigation of this nature before during your days on the police force in Gatlinburg, Tennessee."

Tension tightened in Heath's gut. "That's right."

"Although you were cleared of any guilt you walked away from a promising career."

"I did." He scarcely kept the rest of what he wanted to say in check. What the hell did his past matter? What did it have to do with here and now?

"Then you're aware a certain level of intimidation is necessary to accomplish the mission."

The impulse to grind his teeth was irresistible. Oh yeah, this guy read minds all right. He'd known exactly what Heath had been thinking this morning. "I'm aware that people in your position appear to think so."

Danes's mouth quirked with a less than polite smile. "Touché, Mr. Murphy."

Heath considered briefly whether he should relax or get worried. He decided on the former. Cole Danes was only doing what he did best, unsettling his target's piece of mind.

"I understand you've worked a couple of cases with other investigators here at the agency."

Heath nodded. "That's right."

"Good. I spoke with Victoria this morning and she agrees with my decision on the matter at hand."

That announcement surprised Heath. He hadn't figured Danes for the sort who would take advice from anyone, much less seek it out.

Danes pinned him with that laserlike gaze, demanding full attention. "Since this I.A. investigation doesn't actually pertain to you, I intend to put you to work for me."

"Come again?" Heath must have misunderstood. He was brand new here, hadn't worked a single case on his own. Not to mention that Danes clearly saw the I.A. investigation in his past as a black mark whether he said as much or not.

Danes explained, "The only lead I have at the moment regarding Leberman's connection to the Colby Agency is a man named Howard Stephens. Lucas Camp believes Stephens worked closely with Leberman. I need to find this man."

"Okay," Heath said slowly, drawing out the syllables. "What do you know about him?"

"Not very much. He's former military, a black operations unit within the realm of Special Forces. Twenty years ago his family believed he left the military to join the CIA. According to the intelligence Lucas has collected, Stephens's wife died five years ago and he has made the rare appearance to see his only child, a daughter, since. She's the sole link we have to the man."

Heath considered the information for a moment. "Is he still CIA?"

"He never was CIA. According to military records, Howard Stephens died eighteen years ago. We believe that's when he started working for Leberman, but we have no conclusive evidence."

"So the only hope you have for discovering Stephens's whereabouts is through his daughter?" Heath didn't like where this was headed.

"Therein lies the trouble," Danes went on. "She *is* our only link to him—however, I doubt she knows where he is any more than we do. From what I've gathered, he simply shows up from time to time. She never knows when." Another of those utterly fake smiles twisted Danes's lips. "Kind of like a kid waiting on Santa Claus. Sad, wouldn't you say?"

A sickening sort of dread pooled in Heath's gut. He could feel the worst coming. "You're going to use her to find her own father."

"Actually—" Danes leaned forward a bit "—*you* are."

The impact of those three words slammed into

Heath. Every instinct shot to a higher state of alert. "Why me?" He had the least experience of anyone on staff. He understood that he was the only employee exempt where the I.A. investigation was concerned, but surely that alone was not qualification enough for such an important mission. Bottom line: he didn't like this. He had a bad, bad feeling about it. Heath didn't like using people period. Not like this certainly.

Danes shrugged nonchalantly but his expression was anything but casual. "You're the only investigator clear of my suspicion at the moment. You know that."

Heath also knew that there was much more to this decision. A man like Cole Danes would never pin something so important on so little.

"I also know that I'm the least qualified." Heath stated the obvious that Danes appeared to overlook or to skirt. "Being a small-town cop doesn't prepare you for investigations involving guys like Leberman and Stephens. Even homicide detectives don't get the James Bond super-spy course. You want to share the real reason you picked me for this assignment?"

Another of those disingenuous smiles. "Jayne Stephens works as a tour guide and volunteers on a mountain rescue team in Aspen, Colorado. Your mountain-climbing skills are essential."

Ice spread through Heath's chest, freezing everything in its path in a single heartbeat. "If you know as much about me as you think you do," he said tautly, "then you know I don't do that anymore." A dozen painful memories flashed through Heath's mind before he could stop the soul-shattering process. He clenched his jaw and squashed the images. He would not go there.

"That's right." Danes looked thoughtful for a moment. "Your girlfriend fell to her death. It was an unfortunate accident, of course. Those things happen," he offered glibly, "even to the best."

And Heath had been the best. That's what made the whole situation so unbearable. Heath never met a rock face he couldn't scale. He'd stayed in shape more for that hobby than he had for his job as a robbery/homicide detective. It wasn't like there was a lot of crime in his town, but living in a tourist hot spot like Gatlinburg had ensured that he'd met all kinds. A couple of skiers from Utah had changed his life. They'd invited him rock climbing in what they called the real world. Not the kind of uphill hiking he'd done his entire life in the Blue Ridge Mountains of Tennessee, but the vertical treks up the Rockies of the West. The true danger zone. The kind of challenges an adrenaline junkie couldn't resist.

He'd loved it, had lived for the thrill. And then he'd made his one mistake. He'd wanted to share his passion for climbing with the woman he loved. Had told himself he could teach her all she needed to know...could keep her safe.

"You picked the wrong man for the job," he told Danes, his voice strangely emotionless as he dragged himself from the place that still gave him nightmares in the dead of night.

Danes shook his head. "I'm never wrong, Murphy.

Trust me on that." He tossed a file onto Heath's desk. "Study it. You leave tomorrow."

Heath's gaze riveted to the manila folder as if it contained a contagious, deadly virus. He hadn't skied or climbed in three years. Had sworn he would never...

"Let me know if you have any questions."

Heath's attention jerked upward. "Wait."

Danes hesitated at the door, an unmistakable impatience in his posture.

"I'm not sure you understood me," Heath said flatly. "I can't do this." Uncertainty quaked through him, leaving a too-familiar tremor of weakness. It was out of the question. Impossible.

"Fear can be a good thing," Danes told him, "if you use it to feed your determination."

Anger pushed Heath to his feet and he held up both hands, stop-sign fashion. "Just a damned minute." The fury rushed through him, burning away the chill of remembered pain...the regret and fear that ate at him still. Who the hell did this guy think he was? He was playing God here. Messing around with things that were better left alone. "Even if I did agree to do this, which I won't, how the hell do you expect me to get the information from this woman? Howard Stephens is her father. She isn't going to roll over on him without some big-time motivation."

Silence hung in the air for a pulse-pounding second that felt like ten with Danes's relentless glare boring straight through Heath.

"Anyway you have to," Danes told him. "Coerce

her, seduce her—whatever it takes. Just get the information."

Heath shook his head. "You said her father just pops into her life," he argued. "You said yourself she likely has no idea where he is."

"Correct," Danes allowed. "I'm certain she doesn't know his location anymore than we do."

Heath scrubbed at his forehead and the tension nagging there, hating the fact that his hand trembled with the effort. "Then what the hell is the point?"

"I've put the word out that we intend to get to Stephens through his daughter," Danes said bluntly. "I'm certain that will get our target's attention. We shouldn't have to wait long."

A new blast of outrage obliterated all other emotion. "Doesn't that put her directly in the line of fire?" Heath demanded. Who knew what a guy like Stephens would do to protect himself? Surely Victoria Colby-Camp hadn't sanctioned this kind of maneuver.

"Right again, Murphy. She's the only connection we have. The only bait." Danes opened the door but hesitated once more before exiting, that Arctic gaze pressed in on Heath with renewed ferocity. "I would suggest that you get on the case before he has time to react to the news. Blood isn't always thicker than water."

Danes walked out, closing the door behind him with a succinct thud of finality.

Heath could only stand there, trying to get his fury back under control. What kind of man was this bastard?

Obviously the kind willing to risk an innocent life to accomplish his mission.

"Dammit." Heath dropped back into his chair and stared at the folder on his desk. He closed his eyes and forced away the memories that tried once more to resurface. How the hell could he do this? He'd come to Chicago to put the past behind him. He never wanted to think about the mountains again. Never again wanted to see the way his family and friends back home looked at him. It was his fault she was dead. He knew it. They knew it. He hadn't been the same after that. If he had, he'd have picked up on his partner's dirty game before it was too late. But he'd failed there, too.

He'd let the woman he loved down and he'd let the Gatlinburg police department down, as well.

All he wanted now was to start over.

He could talk to Ian or Simon. Maybe get one of them to call Victoria and get something done about this.

Heath braced his forehead in his hands, kneaded the tension throbbing there. Then they would all know the truth about him.

He was a damned coward.

Afraid of a couple of ghosts from his past.

Scared to death he'd make the wrong decisions all over again if presented with a similar scenario.

How the hell was he supposed to do his job when he couldn't get past the fear?

Reluctantly, his fingers trembling in spite of his every effort, he opened the folder. Big green eyes stared back at him. Long brown hair and a smile that, despite being captured in a mere photograph, took his breath away. Jayne Stephens, 24, soon to be 25, he noted. Her birthday was only a few days away. She looked young and innocent, but there was something else in those eyes that Heath hadn't seen in his own for a very long time. Happiness. This young woman had the world by the tail and her whole life ahead of her. She was in love with life. He could see it in her smile...in those incredible eyes. But that wouldn't last long.

She had no idea that her own past was about to come crashing into her present. Could she possibly know who and what her father was? Though Heath didn't get around much to seeing his own parents anymore, they did talk on the phone fairly often. But that was his fault. He'd made the choice not to go back. Yet, no matter how he felt about his past mistakes, he would still do anything to protect his folks.

This woman would be no different.

Heath read her file from cover to cover. Absorbed the details and facts that made Jayne Stephens who she was. Her life was quiet, organized and predictable. She had nothing to hide. Avoided the limelight and always gave credit to her team members rather than herself after a rescue.

Then he did the only thing his conscience would allow, he called the airline and booked himself on tomorrow's earliest flight to Aspen.

He refused to consider what the weather would be like there right now with February making up for January's lack of potency. Lots of snow. Lots of tourists.

Valentine's Day weekend was coming up. Couples just wanting to enjoy a weekend getaway while hard-core skiers and climbers piled into the town like an overdue avalanche.

When he reached the page that outlined his cover profile a laugh choked from his throat. An investigative journalist? Oh yeah, that was perfect. He'd been cleared by the owner of a local guide service, Jayne's boss in fact, to do a piece on the mountain rescue team. He'd have to give Danes one thing, he'd tied up every detail in a neat little bow. The way had been paved with gold bricks for Heath's entrance. All Heath had to do was show up…and pretend that the past didn't matter. That the snow and the mountains hadn't cost him far too much already. He swallowed back the emotion that scaled into his throat.

He needed the Colby Agency. He couldn't fail, couldn't walk away from his first assignment. Even the shrinks would say that it was past time he'd come to terms with the ghosts that still haunted him.

But that didn't make it any easier.

He flipped back to the photograph of Jayne Stephens. He'd much rather stay here and be stuck right in the middle of the maelstrom this I.A. investigation would surely generate than to set foot on a snow-covered mountain.

Heath closed the file and stood. Well, considering that Danes had already put out the word that Jayne Stephens was a target of this investigation, Heath had little choice but to do what had to be done.

Every instinct he possessed warned him that her father would want to make sure she kept quiet about him.

There was no way to gauge what Howard Stephens might be capable of or willing to do to assure his own safety.

Jayne Stephens's quiet, organized life was about to spin out of control.

Chapter Three

Move it or die.

Jayne Stephens plunged forward, climbing at a relentless pace over and through the snow, her snowshoes sinking into fresh powder and dragging at her determined efforts. White was all around her, interrupted only by the occasional fir tree. She focused on the goal: the avalanche beacon that would ultimately save the lives of three trapped climbers.

As team leader, Jayne kept moving, not slowing even as her forty-pound rescue pack dragged at her weary shoulders and the lung-searing cold puffed in and out of her mouth like blasts of frozen fog. The four-man "hasty" team she led would reach the victims first, do what they could and prep for the arrival of the "support" team. The support team, weighted down with a full rescue load, couldn't move as quickly and efficiently through the morning's fresh snowfall. A full twenty-four inches had fallen in the wee hours before dawn, the snow-packed ice beneath making for perfect avalanche conditions. The absolute crappiest conditions for a rescue.

Jayne glanced at the oddly dark sky. More snow would fall. Soon. If they couldn't get those climbers out this morning, they might not make it out at all. The coming storm would force both teams back.

It was the first rule of rescue: Create no new victims.

But Jayne had no intentions of failing those hikers or her team. They would all make it out.

A new rush of adrenaline urged her onward, pushing her body past the point of exhaustion...past the dark timber of subalpine fir. Just a little farther now. Move faster. Push harder. Don't think, just move it.

Despite the fierce cold a line of sweat slid down her neck. All she had to do was make that ridge and rappel over the side to reach the trapped climbers. Assessing health condition and treating anything life threatening was the most pressing order. Then fuel for the body, solid and liquid, both of which she carried in her pack. By the time the support group arrived she and her team would have the victims ready for transport.

Then all they had to do was make it back down to Express Creek trailhead so the helicopter could lift the victims out of here. The rescue teams would walk out if possible. If not—if the brewing storm had blown in— they'd hunker down in a snow cave until the helicopter came back for them after the weather settled. Every member of the team was prepared for waiting out the worst. Clad in Gore-Tex, polypropylene and Nomex protective wear, maintaining body heat wasn't an immediate issue. Still, with the recent heavy snowfall, they were all walking avalanche triggers. The utmost care had to be taken while maintaining an emergency pace.

Jayne leaned into the thirty-mile-per-hour wind and forced another step and then another until she reached the peak at the south end of Richmond Ridge. She stared back at the members of her team. Little dots floated across her line of vision like defects in her corneas. She squeezed her eyes shut for a few seconds to clear them away. Better. The snow would do that…play games with your vision. With the mind, too, if one wasn't careful.

A quick glance over the ridge and relief rushed through her. An upside-down flag, the universal distress signal, showed her exactly where the climbers had dug in. Thankfully the group had possessed the foresight to wear avalanche beacons and to dig in, making a snow cave for protection from the weather, once they'd realized they were beyond climbing out of their predicament. The latter had likely kept them alive through the bitterly harsh night.

"I'm going over," Jayne told Chad, the first member of her team to reach her position.

"Gotcha."

Chad Wade would serve as the "edge man," ensuring the safety rope stayed in place. The safety rope was swiftly rigged along the ground beside the edge of the cliff, then tied to two solid anchors, one being Chad. After anchoring her rappelling rope, Jayne clipped her harness to the safety rope and stepped over the edge into thin air.

She controlled her descent, stopping long enough to prop her feet against the cliff face, then leaned out, almost horizontal, and began the rigorous journey down to the jutting edge where the climbers had taken refuge after one member of their group had fallen. Adrenaline pumping through her veins, Jayne's mind automatically went through the steps she would need to perform once she reached that precarious ledge.

She'd done this dozens of times. No need to be apprehensive. But somehow today felt different. She couldn't shake the uneasiness that increased with every foot she moved downward. She had no way to contact the trapped climbers other than to call out to them when she'd moved a little closer. A call from a cell phone had alerted the sheriff's office that they were in distress and the avalanche beacon had led the rescue team to their position but attempts at further contact via the cell phone had failed. Either the battery had died or…they had.

She wouldn't accept that. She gritted her teeth and pushed the worst-case scenario aside.

The radio strapped to her chest squawked. "You all right down there, Little Boss?"

Jayne couldn't help a smile. She was the only woman on the team. After the men had finally gotten used to having a female among them they'd eventually taken notice of her skill. Now she was second in command, the little boss. It only took one glimpse of her standing alongside the boss, the rescue team's leader, Walt Messina, for anyone to get the joke.

"No problems," she assured her watchful edge man. The other two members of her hasty team would be preparing for the arrival of the support personnel. Litters would need to be lowered if, as she suspected, the victims were unable to be hauled up with a mere harness.

"Mountain rescue!" she shouted downward. "Can anyone hear me?"

When her voice had stopped echoing, silence hung heavily in the frigid air.

Not good.

Almost there.

She readied herself for stepping onto the ledge. It wasn't more than seven or eight feet wide. Nothing but a jutting boulder from the rock face.

Reaching out for footing, Jayne stretched her right leg toward the ledge at the same time she reared her arm back to dig into the wall with a rock pick.

A jerky tug on the line made her freeze. She glanced upward a split second before the abrupt drop. Her heart rocketed into her throat, accompanied by the whiz of nylon and steel as she struggled to slow her fall.

Shouts and curses blasted from overhead.

Jayne grappled with her rope, trying to catch herself. The line rushed through her gloved fists like water pouring through a sieve. She swung her body like a pendulum, aiming for the rock face. Anything to slow her momentum.

She butted the mountain, then dropped another fifteen feet. The line jerked hard and she flopped against the rock face again. She groaned.

Three or four seconds passed before the realization penetrated that she'd stopped plummeting downward. Her heart sank back into her chest and started beating once more.

"Jayne, you okay?" Carl Brownfield's frantic voice rattled over the radio.

"Yeah, yeah." She sucked in a shuddering breath. Damn, that was too close. "I'm good. What the hell you guys doing up there?"

"The brake failed."

No kidding. Another deep, bolstering breath and she was ready to start the ascent required to regain the ground she'd lost.

"We're gonna haul you up, Little Boss." Chad's re-assuring voice vibrated across the airwaves. "Just keep your balance. We've gotcha."

"Make sure you don't turn loose," Jayne offered with as chipper a tone as she could muster. Her edge man's strained chuckle told her she wasn't the only one nervous here, but she was the one suspended a few thousand feet above the ground. She stole a glance downward and shivered. Long ways down.

As she moved upward her attention returned to the trapped climbers. No response yet. There was always the possibility that they couldn't hear her through the thick, insulating cave of snow.

"Mountain rescue! Can anyone hear me?" she called as she grabbed onto the ledge.

"Paul is on his way down," echoed from the radio.

Jayne glanced upward long enough to acknowledge

that EMT Paul Rice was rappelling down to join her. She hoped like hell his services would be needed…she wanted this to be a live-victim rescue not a body recovery.

Jayne dug into the fresh snow that covered the small cave opening. "Mountain rescue," she repeated, her voice strained with equal measures exhaustion and determination. "Can anyone hear me?"

The sound was very nearly inaudible. A moan or sigh. But it was all she needed to resurrect hope. A gloved hand reached out to her and she smiled through the tears blurring her vision.

Thank God.

THE RETRIEVAL TOOK nearly two hours and the new storm had blown in before they were finished hauling the injured climbers from the ledge. Two of the men suffered from mild hypothermia, but the third man, the one who had initially fallen, was far worse. The various scrapes and bruises were nothing. The real problem was a flail chest—possible broken ribs with fluid buildup. This man would die if he didn't receive medical attention in a hurry.

Jayne and Paul, with the help of two from the support team, rushed the injured man to the waiting helicopter as quickly as possible with the wind and snow blinding their every step. With the victim's condition deteriorating rapidly the helicopter had no choice but to go without the other two. The rescue team would carry the remaining victims out on litters. It wouldn't be easy nor would it be the first or the last time that kind of rescue would be necessary.

The best they could hope for was that everyone would survive.

Jayne pushed harder, sending up a silent prayer as her body strained to obey her commands. *Please God, no new victims.*

NIGHT HAD SETTLED over Aspen like a velvet, snow-capped blanket by the time the day's adventure was truly behind Jayne and the other members of mountain rescue. Coming down was like surfacing from a deep-sea scuba diving journey, the sense of returning to a different world. Home…but not quite. It would be hours, maybe days before the sensation passed.

With the battle between man and nature and the race against time behind her, real life slowly came back into perspective. Her job as a backcountry trail guide, from which she would now be on hiatus until the elevated avalanche advisory had been lifted. Her tiny apartment above the Altitude Bar and Grill in the middle of downtown.

Here she was just another face in the crowd of locals who made a living off the thousands of tourists who flocked to the little resort town during the skiing season.

Statements had been given to the reporters who always showed up to cover rescues. The adrenaline was fading and bone-melting exhaustion had set in.

And still the victory party roared on. Rafe Gonzales,

the owner of the Altitude Bar and Grill, provided steak, the trimmings and beer for all involved in the treacherous rescue. The camaraderie was nice, but about the only thing Jayne really wanted to do was slip into a steaming hot tub and then sleep like the dead. Rafe was having none of that. And he was right, she supposed. She did need to eat. Fuel her body to have the strength to make it through a bath before collapsing in bed.

"I thought you were a goner there when that brake failed," Chad said to her as he leaned close and offered his beer mug for a toast.

She managed a faint laugh. "Me, too."

"I should have kept a better check on the equipment." His face had turned far too solemn. He clearly blamed himself for the incident. Like man, things created by man failed from time to time. No one was perfect.

"It happens, Chad." She clinked her mug to his. "Equipment fails. Some things just can't be foreseen. Don't beat yourself up."

Paul Rice dropped into a vacant chair at their table. "He's gonna make it," he announced before taking a long draw from his beer.

"Good." Jayne knew he meant the climber with the flail chest. "He was damn lucky."

"Damn lucky," Chad echoed.

They were all damn lucky.

Jayne finally allowed herself to relax as she watched her teammates do the same. The day had been hell, the weather seriously evil. But they had rescued the victims and hadn't created any new ones. In the end, that was all that mattered.

She ate, drank a couple more beers and then said her good-nights. She was dead on her feet. Had to call it a night or go to sleep right there on the table in spite of the music and the crowd of revelers. The guys gave her the usual ribbing, calling her a sissy but tonight she didn't care—didn't even bother retaliating. She'd get them for it later. Mountain rescue teams underwent periodic training, intensive training. Whenever Walt couldn't be there, she was in charge. They would pay. A smile slid across her lips. Oh, how they would pay.

Jayne trudged through the storeroom and up the backstairs to the second floor. The upstairs portion of the building had been renovated years ago into two apartments. A large one that took up most of the floor space for the owner and his wife who had passed away a couple of years ago. And the second into a mother-in-law suite. But the mother-in-law was long gone, too. Rafe was all alone now. He and his wife had never had children so the extra room was rented out. Jayne had moved in three years ago and had never left.

The place provided all that she needed. She opened the door and went inside, not bothering to lock it. She didn't have to worry about security. Rafe had a state-of-the-art system on the first floor for after hours. During opening hours the kitchen and bar staff made sure no unauthorized persons entered their territory.

Jayne liked it here. She'd spent most of her time until age twenty-one either in chilly Chicago or sunny

California and, in her opinion, Colorado was the perfect balance. Nice summers with amazing winters. The white-capped mountains were awesome all year round. She adored the feel of small-town living in Aspen, though when the tourists and seasonal dwellers arrived the population more than quadrupled.

After her mother's death she'd stayed in California a while but eventually she'd needed a change and this had been it. Becoming a member of mountain rescue had given her the physical and mental challenge she had longed for but hadn't been able to find. Apparently she was an adrenaline junkie just like her father. Living on the edge, surviving danger appeared to be the only obsession that satisfied her lust. Too bad she couldn't share that with anyone. Most of the time it didn't bother her, but once in a while when the guys would start talking about their families, she felt a little left out. She always got over it. That was a lesson she'd learned long ago.

Don't dwell on things you can't change.

When the tub brimmed with steaming water she peeled off the layers of Nomex and Gore-Tex and long underwear. The soothing water welcomed her like a lover. In fact she couldn't imagine any man giving her the satisfaction that the hot, enveloping embrace a long, hot soak offered. But then, she was a little cynical when it came to men. Not men in general, just lovers and husbands.

She'd watched her mother waste away, in love with a man who was more apparition than husband. Jayne's first love affair had ended badly in college, mainly because she had managed to maintain a higher grade point average and get through her classes faster, ultimately leaving him behind. Men didn't like to be outdone it seemed. Maybe that's what had gone wrong the last time, as well. The man she'd thought was special apparently hadn't been able to deal with her rescue work. So, like her old college beau, he'd dropped out of her life without so much as a goodbye. Poof…he was gone.

Still, there were men in her life. Her father, though she saw him only rarely. She'd long ago forgiven him for basically deserting her and her mother. He had done and still did what he had to do. Her teammates. She cared deeply for each one, respected them all as equals. But even among those fine men she saw the primal beasts that roared beneath their civilized exteriors. They loved the adrenaline rush of a rescue, would risk life and limb regardless of wives and children at home. They would take days on end off work to go on a rescue, ensuring a constant state of financial chaos.

But how could she hold against her teammates the very defect she recognized in herself? She couldn't. Though to her credit, she didn't have a spouse or children. Probably never would. Jayne frowned. How did one trust anyone that much? Love was one thing, because she certainly loved her father, cared deeply for her teammates, Walt and Rafe. She smiled at the thought of her landlord who was more family than friend. The crusty old man was like an uncle to her. Her only family actually since she so seldom saw her father. Loving a man wasn't the real problem, it was the "in" love thing, she supposed.

Trust was an altogether different animal. She trusted the team and her close friends here. She just wasn't sure she could trust anyone with her whole heart and her body. Sex was nice, but falling "in" love…hmm…she'd have to think about that sometime when she wasn't totally exhausted.

Or never.

She didn't need a husband to be complete.

Jayne Stephens was happy.

She drew in a deep, contented breath and sank deeper into the water. Her life was as close to perfect as one could get. She lived in the perfect town, had great friends who didn't get into her business. What else could she ask for?

Pushing away the hint of doubt that lingered, she washed her hair and soaked a while longer before reluctantly dragging her wholly relaxed body from the cooling water. She wrapped her dripping hair in a towel then pulled on her ancient terry cloth robe without bothering to dry off. She'd draped the robe over the radiator to warm it while she soaked. The heat wrapped around her now, making her moan appreciatively.

Hot cocoa. That would be the ultimate ending to the evening. Then she planned to sleep for at least twelve hours. It would be days before the avalanche advisory would be lifted and that gave her a nice break from work. Maybe she'd even get to spend her birthday doing something totally frivolous like shopping.

Twenty-five. She shuddered. Somehow that sounded *so* old. Pushing the thought away, she reminded herself that she was still twenty-four…at least for a couple more days.

She filled the kettle with water and lit the stove eye. A hefty mug, a couple of marshmallows and one-fourth cup of milk added in for richness and she'd be in business. The cocoa might be instant but she'd learned how to doctor it up making it taste almost as good as the pricey concoction they offered at the coffee shop across the street.

A soft rap on her front door drew her there. The kitchen and living room were one fairly spacious room. A tiny hall opposite the front door led to her bedroom and bathroom, which were admittedly cramped. Despite the lack of actual square footage, the soaring, beamed ceilings of the ancient architecture and the massive front window overlooking snow-laden sidewalks and twinkling storefronts made the place at once cozy and chic.

Jayne pulled the door open without identifying the visitor. This was a close community, everyone knew everyone else.

Walt Messina, the rescue team's commander-in-chief—so to speak—and her boss at Happy Trails, towered in her doorway.

"I heard about the brake failure," he growled. Walt was like a big old bear. But, to those who knew him well, he was all bark and no bite. Another man she felt intensely fond of.

She nodded. "Gave me a bit of a scare but Chad took control of the situation." She opened the door wider and stepped back for her boss to come inside.

He shook his head. "I don't want to intrude." He noted her robe. "Just needed to ask a favor of you."

Jayne's senses went on alert. Walt didn't ask for favors, he gave orders, generally without justifying them first. For the second time today a sense of things not being right nudged her.

"What's up?" She propped against the door, her weary legs reminding her she'd been through a lot today.

Walt stared at the floor a moment. "Well, I've got an old friend at the *Denver Post* who needs something from me."

Jayne raised her eyebrows in question. She hadn't a clue what this could have to do with her but obviously her boss did. "You're originally from Denver, right?" she asked for lack of anything else to say.

He bobbed his head up and down. "He wants a real-life piece on the life of a trail guide and a mountain rescue member. Says it's real important to his publisher."

Jayne shrugged. "You don't want to give him the interview?" Sounded like an easy fix to her. A frown inched its way across her brow at his hesitation to answer her question. Judging by Walt's expression there wasn't anything easy about it.

After several moments of deliberation, he confessed, "He doesn't want it from me. He wants a woman's perspective."

It took a few moments for the words to infiltrate the nice little buzz the beer she'd had for dinner and the relaxing bath had cloaked around her brain. "A woman?" she parroted. He couldn't mean…

"I need you to do this for me, Jayne. I owe this guy."

Her head was moving from side to side of its own volition before the words were fully out of her boss's mouth. "I don't need some reporter dragging around in the snow with me, Walt. You have to know what an added risk that would be. You know the rule *don't create any new victims.* You're the one who came up with that slogan."

He hung his head. "I know. But I'm desperate here. This is important. Can you help me out?"

She crossed her arms over her chest and rolled her eyes. "For how long?" She had to be out of her mind to agree to this. If she didn't love her big old cuddly boss so much she'd tell him to forget it. But clearly this was a big deal to him. He either owed this guy big-time as he said or he wanted to impress him by showing off a member of his team. A *female* member, which was admittedly a rarity.

"Three days tops," he said quickly. "As soon as the avalanche advisory passes you can take him on a private tour of whatever peak you prefer."

She lifted one eyebrow skeptically. "Can this guy even ski? I'm not risking my life so some lowlander can scramble up a mountain. He'd better be a skilled climber or he can forget hiking up any peak that would interest me."

Walt blushed to the roots of his gray hair. What was up with that?

"He…ah…he's a skilled climber," her boss assured her. "Has a lot of experience. He won't be a liability."

Jayne still wasn't convinced. "I'll be the judge of that," she countered, annoyed. "He'll have to pass a competency test before he goes anywhere with me." There. That should scare off the cocky reporter. She felt certain once her boss explained to the guy just exactly what a competency test involved he'd be ready to high-tail it back to Denver.

Walt suddenly stepped to one side and another man came into view. Jayne's heart skidded to a near stop. Tall was the first detail her mind wrapped around. Dark hair and eyes…the darkest brown eyes she'd ever seen. And those dark orbs were glittering with amusement at her at that very moment.

"When would you like to start?" he asked.

The deep, husky sound of his voice shivered over her skin like a gust of summit wind…only it warmed her on the inside while it raised goose bumps on her flesh.

"Er…Jayne, this is Heath Murphy. He's the investigative journalist my friend at the *Post* sent to capture this story." Her boss gestured to the man at his side. "Mr. Murphy, this is Jayne Stephens, the best trail guide and rescuer on my team."

Heath Murphy thrust out his hand. "It's a pleasure, Ms. Stephens."

Her eyes still glued to the mesmerizing ones analyzing her so thoroughly, Jayne placed her palm against the one offered. Something electrical sizzled up her arm setting off alarms in her head. Startled, she jerked back her hand. Her bewilderment instantly morphed into renewed irritation. What the hell was wrong with her? The beer maybe? The weakness left behind after a wild adrenaline rush…whatever the problem she had no intention of acting like a starstruck adolescent.

"I wish I could say the same, Mr. Murphy," she said bluntly. "But you see, in my line of work, the unknown can get you killed."

A smile stretched across that handsome face and her knees almost buckled at the sensual intensity of it. "Don't worry, Ms. Stephens, I can assure you I know how to handle myself in any situation."

Oddly, that was the part that scared her the most.

Chapter Four

A sultry mix of rhythm and blues whined from the speakers tucked neatly into the Altitude Bar and Grill's classic decor. The jukebox filled with classics was set on continual play—the spirits flowed like a river. The place was crowded with impatient skiers infuriated by the avalanche advisory that had kept them off the slopes that day. Threats of skiing tomorrow, whatever the conditions, were tossed about like speculations on the rise or decline of the stock market, with every bit as much vehemence.

Heath shook his head. Stupid tourists. Whether they were skilled skiers or not, getting out in this kind of weather was suicide. Two more feet of snow had been dumped on the area just yesterday, making conditions ripe for trouble. Those who'd doled out the cash for one-week stays in one of the country's premiere ski resorts had a single goal in mind—getting their money's worth. They'd come here for the snow, what was the big deal?

Not smart.

Jayne Stephens had done a stellar job ignoring Heath

for most of the day. He'd watched her leave her apartment practically before daylight to go for a five-mile
run. He had to admit he hadn't gone five miles in a
while. Over the past couple of years he'd gotten kind
of lazy, putting in no more than the perfunctory two or
three miles per day that being a cop required. Just
enough to keep in decent shape.

The cold combined with the altitude hadn't made this
morning's extra effort any easier. Once he'd nearly been
certain she'd noted his presence, but then she'd gone on
as if she'd seen nothing at all.

Still, he had a feeling she'd known he was there.

After a shower and change of clothes she'd moved
on to errands and shopping. She'd dropped by the post
office, cruised a couple of women's boutiques, then
popped in the supermarket. She'd parked her decade-
old SUV behind the bar and trudged up the back stairs,
both arms loaded with bags of groceries.

She hadn't come out of her room again until
5:00 p.m. when she'd joined Rafe in the bar to work.
That move had surprised Heath. He hadn't read anything in her file about her working at the bar and grill
from time to time, but according to Rafe she helped him
out fairly often. Good help was hard to find, he insisted.
His best waitresses were always leaving town with
some rich tourist.

Considering every waitress Heath had seen thus far
was not only young but attractive, he could see that
happening. He wondered what kept Jayne Stephens
hanging around. He sipped his beer and watched her

now. Her thick brown hair was pulled back into a braid that hung to her waist. Those green eyes were attentive and the smile…well, the smile was pretty damned gorgeous. Every male in the room noticed, even those accompanied by a wife or girlfriend.

The only person who didn't seem to take note of the attention was Jayne herself. She stayed busy, never slowing or taking extra time to chat. He wondered at that. A young, attractive woman like her should have a steady social calendar, but from what he'd learned so far she scarcely dated and hadn't had a single long-term romantic interest since her arrival in Aspen three years ago.

She took her work seriously, too seriously maybe. Appeared to have no interest in pursuing anything beyond the degree in geology she'd already achieved.

Content.

A frown tugged at Heath's brow. That was the word. Jayne Stephens seemed content with her life just as it was. Definitely unusual this day and time. Satisfaction was a difficult state to reach and maintain. Even he couldn't call himself content. There were holes in his life, past and present. A kind of emptiness haunted him that never really went away.

Heath took a sip from his beer and pushed the thought away. The past was gone…dead. No point rehashing any of it.

Work was what he did now. The occasional date accompanied by sex and then nothing. Eventually he'd stopped bothering, focusing solely on getting a new career off the ground. He had reason to cut himself some slack. He wondered what was her issue. She had to have one. People didn't turn off certain needs without a reason.

"Okay."

The subject of his reverie dropping into the chair across the table from him jerked Heath from his unsettling musings. His gaze clashed with hers before he could completely disguise his surprise at her sudden move.

"Why are you watching me, Mr. Murphy?" She placed her tray on the table and propped her elbow next to it to rest her chin in her hand. Those clear green eyes studied him with a curiosity that was at once disconcerting and appealing.

He gave himself a mental shake. "Heath. Call me Heath."

She leaned back in her chair and studied him a bit longer before continuing. "All right. Heath. Why are you watching me like this? I thought you were here to cover mountain rescue or hiking in the backcountry. What does my waiting tables have to do with either of those things?"

"I'm interested in all aspects of your life. This—" he gestured to the room at large "—is part of what makes you who you are."

She cocked her head and eyed him skeptically, apparently searching for the ulterior motive. "Really?"

Cute, he decided, even annoyed as she was. "Absolutely."

Jayne pushed to her feet and picked up her tray. When she would have walked past him to attend to her customers she leaned down and whispered in his ear, "Just one pointer—you're going to have to run a hell of a lot faster if you plan to keep up with me."

A self-deprecating grin slid over Heath's lips. Oh yeah. She'd noticed him this morning. He watched her move back to the bar to place an order but this time his attention wasn't drawn to her long hair…those swaying hips snagged his complete interest. He wasn't supposed to focus on those kinds of details, but she had a great body. Running wasn't all she did to keep in shape, he'd wager. A little body pump, maybe yoga for flexibility. A person, man or woman, had to have tremendous upper-body strength to be a climber, especially one trained to rescue the injured.

Her legs were long, well muscled but still womanly. Very nice curves—dangerous curves—completed her stature. This morning's running attire had included frame-forming material from the waist down. Great legs, great ass. Both of which he could objectively appreciate as a man, he told himself. The assessment was a fact, nothing more.

She turned just then and objectivity went out the window. His heart rate surged as if he'd just scaled to some unseen peak. What was it about her innocent beauty that disturbed him so? She could very well be hiding information about her father. She could know exactly where he was, who he was, everything.

But the sharpest instincts Heath possessed refuted

that conclusion. She didn't know what her father did...had no idea who he was. Her life was far too serene to be hiding a secret that unsettling. If this mission played out the way Danes wanted it to she would soon learn both things about her father. Maybe that was the part that got to Heath. Her life of simple contentment was about to end and his participation represented the catalyst.

As a police detective he had used people, generally dirtbags, to glean the information he needed. He'd hurt people, even killed once. All in the line of duty.

But never, not once in his life had he damaged the innocent. And this time there was no way around it. He clenched his jaw and stared hard at his glass of beer. If he could find anything on her, some wrong thing she'd done, some knowledge of wrongdoing she possessed, his conscience might just let him slide on this one, but his gut told him that wasn't going to happen.

She was clean.

Innocent.

He closed his eyes and exhaled.

Whatever it takes.

Cole Danes expected him to use her no matter the circumstances or the fallout.

Heath opened his eyes and asked himself the question he should have asked before he surrendered to this assignment.

Would Victoria Colby-Camp have allowed this underhanded strategy? Would she have directed him to use this young woman in whatever way necessary? Heath didn't know Victoria very well but he understood one thing with complete certainty: Victoria was a woman of principle. One who would never compromise those principles. So, the real question was, just who was Heath actually working for? The Colby Agency or Cole Danes?

He had his orders.

She, his gaze followed Jayne as she weaved her way through the congested tables, was his assignment. Whatever it took to reel in her father. No questions, no hesitation. Her emotional well-being would be part of the collateral damage, but Heath would do everything within his power to see that she didn't lose anything else. Keeping her safe, maintaining control over her physical well-being, was paramount.

As she headed back to the bar with an empty tray a rowdy patron snagged her by the arm. Heath went on instant alert, sat up a little straighter. He'd noticed this guy flirting with her all evening. The jerk stood, taking the tray from her and setting it aside as a new, achingly slow R & B melody floated through the air.

Smiling politely, Jayne attempted to beg off the un-wanted advances, but her pursuer didn't let go. Heath pushed to his feet as the jerk tugged her to the dance floor. It was clear that she had grudgingly relented to the dance to prevent a scene.

Before he realized he'd even moved, Heath was at the guy's back, fury pounding in his skull. He tapped him on the shoulder.

"Get lost," the guy tossed over that same shoulder.

In one fluid motion Heath gripped the man's arm and turned him around. Before the jerk could spit out whatever he'd intended to say, Heath warned, "This is my dance, pal."

The lethal intensity of the words sent the guy staggering back a step. "Whatever," he muttered. He released his hold on Jayne and shuffled back to his table and friends.

She looked as annoyed at Heath as she was at the other guy. "It wasn't a big deal," she protested. "Rafe would have stepped in if he'd thought I needed help."

One glance at the bar told Heath she was right. Rafe was watching, his gaze narrowed suspiciously even now.

Heath shrugged. "Looked like a big deal to me."

When she would have walked away Heath stopped her with a hand on her arm careful to keep his touch gentle. "You mean after all that I don't get the dance." He couldn't say what possessed him to make such a move. Maybe Danes's words about seduction echoing in his brain, or maybe just plain old lust. Whatever the case, he wanted this dance…wanted to hold her like that.

She surveyed her tables and tossed a look at her boss before meeting Heath's gaze. "Sure." She halfheartedly hung her arms around his neck and gave him a look that said she had better things to do. "I wouldn't want you to miss out on anything that makes me tick."

Oh, the lady had an attitude problem. He smiled, slid his arms around her waist and scooted her real close. She gasped, startled by the bold move. Heath's smile widened to a grin. "Thanks. That'll make my job a lot easier."

The dance floor was crowded, which ensured that they stayed close. The music drowned out all else. After about thirty seconds Heath gave up on pretending the dance was about the case. Instead, he lost himself to the sweet smell of her. Lilac. Not perfume. Bath oil maybe. Or shampoo. Soft and subtle. Sweet and enticing. He inhaled deeply, allowing her scent to permeate his senses.

The heat…the response she generated in his body surprised him, caught him completely off guard. The man-woman thing, physical attraction. That's all it was. Basic chemistry. But the conclusion didn't ebb the tension tightening inside him. If anything, the mental denial only pushed him closer to some crazy edge on a physical level.

Another couple bumped into them and Jayne's arms tightened around him. His own reacted in kind. Protective instinct, he told himself. But when his jaw brushed her soft temple he knew his speculations were way off course. Want seared through him, burning down too many defenses for comfort.

It was crazy but he couldn't stop it. She felt good in his arms and somehow he needed that. Like going shopping without having eaten for days and buying everything in the supermarket. He felt starved for just this kind of touch…her touch. No strings, no emotional luggage. Just the simple pull of attraction. He hadn't realized how badly he'd wanted to feel that again.

Impossible, the voice of reason insisted…but every sway of her body, every touch of her against him shook him up inside…made him want her more. Incredible…but true. His hands slid down her back, pulled her closer still. He felt the little hitch in her breathing…felt her tremble. And then he stopped, unable to do anything but look at her and wonder at how a total stranger could make him react so irrationally.

The music faded away and she stepped back, her eyes round with surprise or something on that order.

"I have to get back to work."

She left him standing there…watching her walk away.

Heath shook off the haze of lust and made his way back to his table. What the hell had just happened?

He looked at his empty beer mug and decided another was in order but damned if he'd risk having her get close enough for him to order one.

He pushed a path through the thickening crowd, slid onto the one empty bar stool and waited for Rafe to notice his presence. The bar was a sharp contrast to the tables behind him. Most of the folks seated on the stools spoke quietly to each other or basically peered silently into their drinks. The rabble-rousers and dancers were all taking up space around the numerous tables.

He gave himself a mental kick for going stupid on that damned dance floor. Maybe he'd just gotten caught up in the moment. Everyone else was partying the night away.

Yeah, right. And maybe he'd lost his mind. That was the more likely scenario. Lust. He'd neglected his social life far too long.

Jayne rushed up to the bar a few feet away and belted out an order. Thankfully four or five occupied seats separated her from Heath. He refused to look her way but, as bad luck would have it, their gazes collided in the mirror behind the bar. She looked away first.

Damn.

Twenty-four hours and he'd already lost control of the game. Not a good sign for his future career. He had a feeling Cole Danes was not the sort of man who readily accepted failure.

Rafe placed an icy mug of brew on the counter in front of Heath. "You look a mite unsettled, Mr. Murphy. Is everything all right?"

So they were back to Mr. Murphy. This morning the old guy had been pleased to be on a first-name basis.

"Everything's great," Heath allowed, pinning a smile into place.

Rafe propped on the counter and leaned slightly toward him. His words were spoken just loud enough for Heath's ears only. "Look, young fella, I don't know what your game is, but I don't like what I just saw. I thought you came here for a story. I don't like people taking advantage of my hospitality."

"I'm here for the story, nothing more and I would never take advantage of your hospitality."

Whether Rafe saw the sincerity in Heath's eyes or simply decided to leave it at that, he added, "We all have stories, Murphy, but this little gal's like a daughter to me. Don't *write* anything to hurt her."

Heath shook his head adamantly and shimmied his answer somewhere between the God's truth and a flat-out lie. "That's not my intent here."

The older man's analyzing gaze turned hard. "And when you go, don't take anything you didn't bring with you. Got it?"

"Got it."

"She was hurt by a stranger like you a couple years ago, I don't want her to go through that kind of grief again." With that said, Rafe went back to tending bar and Heath drifted back into self-disgust.

Twenty-four hours and he'd lost his perspective.

How the hell had it happened so fast?

JAYNE LOCKED HER apartment door for the first time in a very long time. She sagged against the door and questioned her motives.

It was him. He made her feel insecure…uncertain.

She didn't like that. Didn't appreciate some stranger coming into her life and making her feel…afraid.

Peeling off her T-shirt, she hesitated. Was that all she'd really felt when he'd held her in his arms? She tossed the garment aside. No, that wasn't all she'd felt by any means. Attraction, she'd felt attraction for a man she didn't even know. She pushed off her jeans and shoes. Okay, so it wasn't the first time she'd had the hots for the new guy in town. But that had only happened once and he had, apparently, realized she wasn't the girl for him since he'd left without even saying goodbye.

Would she be smarter this time? Avoiding Heath Murphy would be the smartest thing to do. But that wasn't possible. Her boss wanted her to spend time with Heath Murphy…to give him the story he wanted. She dragged her fingers through her hair, releasing the braid, and allowing the long tresses to fall around her shoulders.

Jayne looked at herself in the mirror and wondered why of all the women in the bar tonight he'd stayed so focused on her. It wasn't like waiting tables would be a pivotal part of his story. Even she knew better than that.

She hadn't been the most beautiful girl there tonight. There had been plenty of uninhibited young ladies who could have shown him a good time for the night. Something resembling jealousy trickled through her.

Jayne laughed at herself. She was taking all this far too seriously. Mr. Heath Murphy would blow out of town just as quickly as he'd breezed in. All she had to do was give him the story he wanted and then he'd vanish. The last thing she needed to do was let him take a chunk of her heart when he left.

With a sigh, she stripped off her bra and pulled on a nightshirt. Trust was something she gave only to her rescue team members. She couldn't trust this guy. No matter how innocuous his reasons for wanting to hang around her. There was always a chance…

The telephone rang, derailing the one subject she'd

put off dealing with. She preferred to stay away from that place. It hurt too much to even consider the possibility.

"Hello."

The silence on the other end of the line sent her heart into a faster rhythm.

"Jayne."

A rush of affection soared through her, overshadowing the doubt and uncertainty.

"Dad!" She sank onto the side of her bed and leaned against the mound of pillows. "It's so good to hear from you." A part of her would never understand why he couldn't manage to visit more often, or at least call on a regular basis, but when he finally did call or visit it made the whole wait worth it.

"How's my girl?"

She suppressed a sigh. He had no way of knowing just how close *blue* came to describing her mood tonight. "Fine. And how are you?"

The pause before his answer made her frown. "I'm good, honey. As always."

This time she was the one who paused to analyze his tone, the words he used. Not nearly as jolly as usual. Definitely not his customary choice of verbal play.

"I missed you at Christmas," she admitted, feeling as petulant as a five-year-old. This was the first time for as long as she could remember that he'd missed calling on a holiday.

"Sorry about that. I was out of the country. Couldn't be helped."

Work. Her father's work kept him from sharing his actual job description with her. But she'd read between the lines and seen enough movies to put two and two together. He was undoubtedly a spy of some sort. Probably for the CIA since he spent so much time out of the country. Her mother had concluded as much, but neither of them had ever really known. He neither confirmed nor denied their conjecture.

"But I promise I'll make it up to you. Soon."

Her fallen expression lifted. Making up usually involved a visit. She hadn't seen him in…more than a year. A visit would be terrific.

"When?" He had to hear the anticipation in her voice. She was such a child whenever he called. It was like twenty years ago all over again. His every call, every visit was like Christmas any time of the year. Even when he'd stopped coming at all for months on end, sometimes years, she still anticipated his arrival like most children did Santa Claus or the Tooth Fairy.

But it hadn't been the same for her mother. She'd heard her mother talking with friends. Had heard her use the word desertion in connection with her father. Had watched her mother steadily grieve herself into an early grave. Yet, Jayne couldn't stop loving her father, not even for his past sins. She had no one else. No siblings, no cousins she knew of. No one. He was all she had left in the world. And she had every intention of hanging on until the end.

Besides, her father was fifty-five. Retirement had to be right around the corner. He'd promised to retire here.

In Aspen where they could spend his twilight years together. She pictured the strong man her father was and somehow twilight just didn't fit.

"I need a favor of you, Jayne."

The subtle change in the nuances of his tone set her on edge. Something was wrong. She hadn't heard him sound like this in years…not since he disappeared that one time. And back then she hadn't heard from him for a whole year after that tense conversation. She'd only been six at the time but she remembered it vividly. She remembered the tears as well. Not hers. Her mother's. Night after night for months she'd heard her mother crying through the thin walls of their home. And then there had been the hasty move to California, as if staying one more day in Chicago would have been too risky.

"Sure, Dad, anything."

"I want you to be very careful. Especially now. Remember I've always told you that I have enemies." She nodded but, of course, he didn't see her, but he knew she understood. "I've always been able to keep you separate from that unpleasant business but I'm not sure I've managed this time. *This time is different.*"

Jayne sat up, her pulse skittering as much from his tone as from his words. "What do you mean?"

"There are people who want to hurt me and they will do anything to get to me." A heavy breath hissed across the line. "Including using you, I fear."

"They know about me?" Fear trickled through her veins. She moistened her lips and bit it back. She would not be afraid. Her father had taught her to be stronger than that. He'd kept her a secret and she'd done the same. It was the safest way.

"I have reason to believe that they do." Another unsettling pause. "I hate to have to do this to you, honey, but I would feel a lot better if you got out of there. I'd like to stash you away some place safe for a while."

The grown-up Jayne warred with the obedient daughter who still lived for these rare and precious moments. "But, Dad, I can't do that. I—I have commitments."

"I know you do, that's what makes the request so difficult, but it would mean a great deal to me if you could indulge me this once."

This once.

Hard as she tried Jayne couldn't help resenting that statement. She and her mother had indulged him for a lifetime. How could he use her emotions against her? She loved him, desperately, but this wasn't right. To ask her to do this—to possibly give up everything—it just wasn't fair. These phone calls, rare visits were all he'd ever given her and she clung to them. But this was too much. Even she, despite the child deep inside her who would do most anything for his approval, recognized the injustice of this request.

"Dad, you know I love you and I'd love to help. Really I would, but I can't do this. You're asking too much. As soon as the avalanche advisory is lifted I'll be in the backcountry twenty-four/seven."

Her soul ached, cried out for her to take back the words, but she held her tongue, stayed strong. She couldn't do this, not even for her father.

He chuckled softly. "I thought you might say that. So, I'll ask you to at least do one thing for your old man."

Relief gushed through her with such force that it momentarily stole her voice. She simply couldn't bear being on the outs with him. No matter how little impact he'd had on her everyday life, their connection was a powerful one.

"What would that be?" she ventured, her voice warbling, giving away the emotion she so wanted to shield from him.

"Take extra care in all that you do. Beware of any strangers who come into your life."

She smiled through the tears crested on her lashes. "You know I always do that, Dad, but I promise to be extra careful."

"Good. Just one last thing—"

"You mean there's more?" She swiped at her eyes, her heart aching to beg him for the whole truth. Something was very, very wrong. She was an adult now, why couldn't he tell her the truth?

"No matter what anyone tells you, Jayne, always, always remember that I love you."

And then, with a simple click, he was gone.

Jayne stared at the receiver for a long while after that. He'd called to warn her. He was in trouble. It didn't take someone in the secret agent business to figure that one out. He was in deep trouble and he feared for her life.

Beware of any strangers who come into your life.

At the moment there was only one stranger in her life....

Chapter Five

"He made contact."

"I know."

Heath had thought he was prepared for this exchange but he'd been wrong.

"You know?" How could Cole Danes know before Heath reported in?

"The place is wired, Murphy. Do you think I'd leave anything to chance? That's not my style."

He should have anticipated that, Heath thought scathingly. He should have and he hadn't.

A man like Danes covered all bases up front. "In that case, is there some point to my being here?" Heath returned, irritated that he hadn't been told about this in the mission briefing—if one could call the demand that he take this assignment a briefing.

"Your job, as you well know, Murphy, is to keep our bait viable until we have what we need."

Rage burned its way through Heath's gut. "Not to worry, Danes," he shot back, allowing his irritation to show, "that's my primary mission. I won't be letting anything happen to our *asset*."

"I'm sure you won't. He'll be close now. He knows you're in place. She may be suspicious of you for that reason."

Heath resisted the impulse to suggest that Danes had likely given Stephens his name and description just to be sure the man recognized the enemy in a timely enough manner. But he kept his mouth shut. He had a job to do. He couldn't let his distrust of Danes interfere with that job.

"You know what I need," Danes reminded before ending the call.

"Yeah, I know," Heath muttered to himself as he closed the phone and tossed it onto the bedside table. He liked this guy less and less. Cold and relentless is what he was, that much was crystal clear. Uncaring about who he hurt to accomplish his mission. Heath hadn't signed on to work with men like Cole Danes.

But the internal affairs investigation would be over soon. If Danes got what he needed from Stephens then perhaps the Colby Agency could return to normal. Again he couldn't help wondering how Victoria felt about all this. If Heath was unhappy with the situation he could only imagine how the woman who'd turned the Colby Agency into the thriving, well-regarded firm it was today felt.

Heath studied the image on his laptop. Jayne worked hard and slept the same way. She hadn't moved a muscle since she'd climbed into bed two hours ago. He'd situated the monitors in her apartment to cover all doors and windows, had installed a listening device on her landline as well as her cell phone. His monitoring of her activities would be strictly on the up and up, allowing her the privacy she deserved when she undressed or bathed. To take advantage of a situation like this would be reprehensible. His observations were for her safety, not for his carnal pleasure. Admittedly, the desire to study her every move for more than simply business had flared more than once, but he'd squashed it without hesitation. He wasn't that kind of man. She needed his protection, not his lust.

He closed his eyes and thought of the sweet expression on her face when she'd spoken to her father. That call had thrilled her. She loved the man. Missed him. Didn't suspect for a moment that he was a bad guy. Her eyes had shone brightly with emotion. After she'd hung up the phone, she sat for a while, hugging her arms around her knees, looking as vulnerable as the little girl Stephens had literally abandoned nearly two decades ago.

She'd needed a father then, needed him even now. Heath slowly moved his head from side to side. No wonder she looked at the owner of the bar and grill like an uncle, and the guys on her rescue team like family. She needed that male influence in her life to make up for the past…for the one man she'd longed for all these years. Heath now knew with certainty that her father was the reason she'd avoided long-term romantic commitment. Trusting her male friends was one thing, but she wasn't about to give another man her heart; the single most important male figure in her life had already broken it.

What a waste.

Those feelings of protection had welled inside a hundredfold as Heath watched her sleep. But there was no way to make his part in this right. Howard Stephens was guilty of the unthinkable, the worst of which included helping to steal Victoria Colby-Camp's son and torturing him for nearly twenty years. The bastard was evil incarnate in Heath's opinion with only that one black mark against him. But there was more. He and Leberman had killed Victoria's first husband, James Colby. The small group of mercenaries that had once operated within Leberman's dominion had to be stopped once and for all. That couldn't happen without cutting off the head of that poisonous viper, Stephens.

Jayne would be devastated when she learned who and what her father was. If Heath had possessed any doubt about her innocence in this, it was undeniable at this point. He would be the deliverer of that horrible truth. She would hate him for it. Her life would never be the same.

Fury swept through Heath all over again at the thought of the call from Danes. That her every move and word was funneled into Heath's laptop hadn't bothered him because he performed his job with the utmost respect. Would not take advantage of the opportunity. But the idea that Danes might be watching as well as listening…that bugged the hell out of Heath. Danes had apparently set up the monitoring system's software to live feed both Heath's receiver and one back at the agency. That move was, as he'd so eloquently put it, a part of his "not taking any chances."

Heath blew out a disgusted breath and dropped his feet to the cold floor. No way in hell could he sleep. Somehow he had to put a stop to this obsessing about Danes's character. Heath had a job to do just as Danes had been hired to accomplish a certain mission. He, from all accounts, was very good at doing his particular work. Who was Heath to say if what he did was right or wrong? He didn't have all the facts, Heath told himself as he blew out another heavy breath. The only thing he could do was carry out his mission, which was to protect the asset while luring in the target.

He'd spent too much time already analyzing Cole Danes. Heath had his assignment. He had to remember that things were never completely black and white. Hadn't he learned that lesson the hard way in his last career?

Pushing up from the bed he decided a perimeter check and a snack were in order. No point lying here watching Jayne sleep via the monitor while the likelihood of his sleeping grew more remote.

That was just another thing he had to get back under control.

He had to stop thinking about her as a woman. She was an asset. One who needed his protection. He couldn't stay sharp if he let this case get personal. Maybe he wasn't as ready for his first assignment as he'd thought. He'd spent eight years in law enforcement working cases and doing a hell of a good job keeping objective—what was the problem now? It was this place, he knew. It reminded him too much of the past he wanted to forget…perhaps the setting was throwing him off, making him feel unsure of himself and allowing doubt to take root.

But he was here. End of subject.

Heath slipped from the small room and moved quietly down the short corridor, which led directly into the kitchen of the Altitude Bar and Grill. Rafe had told him to make himself at home in the kitchen when he'd offered the only vacant room within the city limits.

Every hotel, motel and resort cabin in the Aspen area had been booked even before Heath arrived. Ski season was at its peak, not to mention some sort of junior Olympics event was in town. Walt Messina, Jayne's boss and the owner of Happy Trails guide service, had hit up his buddy Rafe for the proverbial "back room." Walt knew Rafe had remodeled the bar's back room into a one-room efficiency when he first took over the establishment. Originally the room had served as a bunk for Rafe's first bartender whenever the snow got too heavy for him to make it up to his cabin or for whenever Rafe was on the outs with his wife of half a lifetime. Nowadays it served mostly as a place for visiting friends to crash when they'd indulged in a little too much of the bar's offerings.

Heath felt confident that Rafe's decision to let him use the room had more to do with his desire to keep an eye on Heath than out of hospitality. The old man was very protective of Jayne. Walt Messina had no reason to suspect Heath since his friend at the *Post* had vouched for him. Of course Heath had never met the gentleman at the *Denver Post* but Cole Danes had. The guy owed him a favor.

Heath scratched his chest as he maneuvered his way through the dark kitchen. He wouldn't want to owe Cole Danes any favors. Heath immediately chastised himself for going back down that road. He had to give Danes a chance, let him do his thing. Trust, or at least patience, was his new watchword. Heath's trust had taken a beating from his former homicide partner, but he couldn't let that disappointment keep him down.

Harsh light blared from the refrigerator when he pulled the door open. Heath blinked against the brightness. He'd been so absorbed in keeping an eye on Jayne tonight he'd failed to eat. But that wasn't unusual. As a police detective he'd always gotten caught up in his cases to the point of letting everything else go.

As he perused the ready-sliced meats and cheeses, he couldn't help wondering what made this time different. Yes, he was fully focused on his asset, but the whole Cole Danes issue kept butting into his perspective. He had to forget that guy and put the I.A. investigation out of his mind. Whatever lurked in the Colby Agency's past had nothing to do with him. This case would be best served if he remembered that fact.

Deli-sliced ham and provolone cheese made his gut rumble. He grabbed the selections as well as the mayo and eased the fridge door closed with one hip. He blinked a couple of times to adjust to the darkness again and set the items on the nearest counter. The overhead light switch was all the way on the other side of the room next to the door leading into the bar. He'd definitely need some light to locate the bread.

The creak of a floorboard alerted him a split second before his gaze zeroed in on movement in the dark near the storeroom door.

He had company.

Heath froze. Let his senses do the work. The intruder moved slowly into the room. There were a couple of exterior windows but tonight's cloud cover ensured virtually no light whatsoever from the moon. A few more steps and his company would be at the end of the long stainless steel island that separated them.

An almost inaudible but sharp intake of breath warned him that his presence had abruptly been noted.

He had to move.

Heath was over the island and on top of the intruder before he could take another step.

The soft scent of lilacs and silky feel of feminine skin exploded in Heath's senses as he pinned the intruder to the cold, steel surface of the counter.

He grabbed something long and solid right before it collided with his head.

Wood.

Baseball bat.

"The police will be here any minute!"

Jayne.

Heath hadn't really needed the threat to recognize her. He'd known who she was the moment he touched her, smelled her. That her lithe body was trapped beneath his against the unyielding steel penetrated his awareness next. As strong as she looked she felt incredibly soft beneath him. Those well-defined and toned muscles were still undeniably feminine, warm and desirable to his touch.

"You'd better let me go you son of a—"

"It's me," he said, cutting her off and jerking himself from the momentary trance he'd drifted into. He pulled the bat from her hand and stepped back. "Heath Murphy."

She whirled away from him and stamped toward the door and the light switch there, the hard slap of her bare feet on the wood floor declaring her fury loud and clear. Oh hell, someone should have told her he was staying here. Obviously it should have been him. He'd assumed Rafe would fill her in.

"What the hell are you doing here?" she demanded as she flipped the switch, flooding the room with fluorescent light. The long bulbs blinked erratically then hummed into full bloom.

Heath looked at the baseball bat he'd wrestled from her then back at the woman. "Do you always wander around in the middle of the night with a deadly weapon?" he teased, hoping to defuse her anger. He laid the bat on the counter, not wanting to look intimidating or threatening in any way.

"Answer the question, dammit." She crossed her arms over her chest and stalked back in his direction.

He wished she had taken the time to don a robe so he wouldn't be distracted by her shapely legs. The nightshirt hit mid-thigh, leaving plenty to derail his concentration. He gave himself a mental shake. It wasn't like he hadn't seen her in that getup already. Somehow the real thing was vastly more appealing than the image on his monitor or maybe he just felt free to appreciate the view when she was aware he was looking.

"I'm staying in the back room." He hitched his thumb in that direction. "The hotels were all booked up. Rafe kindly offered me a place to bunk."

If he'd hoped that assurance would calm her outrage, he'd been wrong. She looked even more furious now.

"Are you telling me," she countered hotly, "that Rafe okayed your staying here and didn't say anything about it to me?"

"Obviously." Heath cleared his throat and gestured vaguely. "I'm sure it was just an oversight. It was a last-minute decision this afternoon and with the busy night in the bar he probably forgot."

"This was Walt's idea, wasn't it?" she accused, those green eyes glowing with ire.

Damn, he could just imagine if all that fury were to morph into another kind of passion…

"Er…yes," he confessed. "Walt suggested it."

Jayne shook her head, none too happy to have her suspicions confirmed, then that sizzling gaze whipped back to his. "You could have mentioned it."

He shrugged, then wrapped his own arms around his chest. He'd never been shy about his body, especially with a woman, but he suddenly felt utterly naked in front of her. He hadn't bothered to drag on a shirt, hadn't expected to encounter anyone.

"I should have, yes." He lifted one shoulder in another apologetic shrug. "I guess I didn't think about it." He let his gaze settle fully onto hers. "I was a little distracted." He didn't have to spell it out...she knew he meant the dance. Recognition flared in her eyes.

Dammit. The impact of his dark eyes was very nearly more than Jayne could bear. She had told herself that he couldn't affect her that way, but she was wrong. He made her shiver in spite of her fury and that only made her angrier.

A new suspicion broadsided her. Her gaze narrowed. "Are you trying to seduce me, Mr. Murphy?" Didn't guys like him always think they could have it all? Just because she was the subject of his story didn't mean she was easy, dammit!

The look of surprise that skittered across that too-handsome face gave her the answer even before he spoke. "No! I..." He looked around as if searching for some better explanation. He pointed to the food he'd dumped on the counter. "I just came in here for a sandwich. I assumed everyone else was asleep."

He was telling the truth. Jayne reasoned that it was her father's call that had unsettled her so, had made her more distrusting than usual. She outright refused to consider that maybe she was simply attracted to the guy and that his overpowering sensuality wasn't really his fault. He was just too damned good-looking. And that hair. Thick and tousled as it was. She wanted to run her fingers through it.

She squeezed her fingers into fists of determination

and resisted the impulse to tap her foot. What the hell
was wrong with her? He might not want to seduce her,
but this guy was still a stranger. She had to remember
her father's warning. She had no way of knowing who
really sent this man. Walt had never even met him before. His name might not even be Heath Murphy. He
could be some sort of spy. A killer maybe.

Yet, her hungry gaze roamed his big, masculine body
once more—he looked utterly adorable right now. A
killer wouldn't look like this…would he?

"Maybe you'd like to join me?" He gestured to the
ham and cheese. "I'd love the company."

It was 2:00 a.m. He had to be out of his mind. Or
maybe she was because she very much wanted to join
him. A pang of hunger sliced through her, but she wasn't
sure ham and cheese would do the trick.

She swallowed back the want that rose in her throat
and tried to relax. "Sure. A sandwich would be nice."
She told herself that the best way to figure out if this
guy was lying to her was to spend more time with
him—question him. See if she could catch him in a lie
or trip him up somehow. But she had an awful feeling
that she was fooling herself.

Walt wouldn't have any friends involved in the spy
or murder business. She joined Heath on the refrigerator side of the island as he found the bread and started
sandwich preparations. She was being ridiculous. He
was just a reporter. A friend of a friend of Walt's. She
trusted Walt. Trusted Rafe. If they liked this guy—
trusted this guy—who was she to argue?

Jayne pushed away her father's nagging warning and decided to do this her own way. If Heath Murphy was here to get at her father or to harm her there was only one way to find out.

When Heath's masterpiece sandwiches were ready for debut and Jayne had filled two glasses with milk, she pulled up an old wooden stool on the opposite side of the counter from him. She wanted to watch his facial expressions as they talked. At least that's what she told herself. It wasn't a hardship, but it was necessary, wasn't it?

She had to know if this guy was for real.

"I've never cared for Denver," she told him bluntly. "Have you always lived there?"

He washed down a mouthful of sandwich with a big swig of milk. "Actually I live in Chicago. I'm a freelance writer so I do articles for a number of publications around the country."

Uneasiness slid through her. "So you don't actually work for Walt's friend?"

He shook his head. "I do but I don't." A slow, easy smile widened that full mouth. "Does that make sense?"

Wow. She blinked, averted her gaze from that megawatt smile. "Yeah, sure." She took a bite of her sandwich to buy some time for contemplating her next question.

"Aspen has always been home to you?" he asked before she could decide on her next move.

"I lived in Chicago until I was six." She supposed that gave them something in common, in a roundabout way. She resisted the urge to roll her eyes. Why in the world would she care if they had anything in common? He was just a minor nuisance in her life that would be gone before she could decide if he was friend or foe.

"Really? Where? Maybe I live in that same neighborhood." He flashed that smile again.

"Oak Park." She remembered the little house they'd owned there. She'd hated the basement. Wouldn't even go down there with her mother. But the neighborhood had been nice enough the best she remembered.

"Do you miss it?" he asked. "Chicago, I mean."

"No." Jayne's appetite vanished. Somehow the subject of Chicago always had that effect on her. Maybe it was because that's where everything had changed. She, her mother and father had lived what felt like the perfect life then. At least, to the extent she could remember. He had come home more often, even stayed for weeks at a time. Her mother had kept the house filled with scents of cookies baking and pot roasts simmering. She'd had lots of friends at school and in the neighborhood.

Then suddenly it all ended. Her father disappeared and she and her mother moved away.

"Earth to Jayne."

She blinked. "What?" She hadn't realized he'd said anything. Nor did she like the way he was looking at her now. Analyzing her. Trying to read between the lines of her answers, as well as her distraction. She was the one who needed to be analyzing. Instead she'd gotten bogged down with the past. She hated when that happened.

"I was asking where you ended up after Chicago."

"Sacramento, California." That her tone still sounded distracted flustered her. Her father's call had her off balance, that's all. She refused to consider that it might be this damnable attraction to the man facing her at the moment. They'd only just met.

She wished now that she hadn't been awakened by his late-night plundering. Somehow her gaze shifted downward from his face, to rest on his bare chest. For a desk jockey he kept in great shape. Those broad shoulders were sculpted much like a climber's. She already knew how strong he was by the way he'd pinned her to this countertop and taken the bat away. She shivered and focused on the barely touched sandwich on her plate.

"I'll bet it took some time to adjust to that kind of change."

Again Jayne found herself scrambling to catch up with the conversation. He'd said more, but the words hadn't penetrated the haze of lust she'd slipped into.

"It wasn't that bad," she lied. She'd hated California. No one had liked her. The school had been so different from the one she'd attended in Chicago that she'd been utterly miserable. That's when she'd started her climbing hobby.

Memory after memory of her climbing high in the trees in her backyard flashed one after the other through her mind. She'd started out being satisfied with reaching the lower limbs, but then the need to go higher and higher had become an obsession. It had been the perfect escape. High above the rest of the world. Looking down on all those who treated her as an outsider.

She'd been in love with climbing ever since.

"I learned a lot about myself there," she said out loud, more to herself than to the man staring expectantly at her. She settled her gaze on his. "I learned I could be anything I wanted to, all I had to do was work at it."

And she had. She'd gotten through school, had herself a degree in geology but never once had she felt inclined to teach or do research. She'd rather just revel in the natural beauty and wonders that God had created. That need for adventure had brought her here. Just for the winter she'd told herself. After college she'd wanted, needed, a break before making a decision on what to do with the rest of her life. Her mother was gone. There was nothing holding her anywhere.

She'd come here that winter for the season and she'd never left. Her hard work and perseverance had paid off. She explored nature's beauty for a living and helped show others what the world at twelve thousand feet above sea level had to offer. It was amazing.

She didn't drive a fancy SUV, just an old clunker she'd picked up from a local. She didn't own her own home. But none of that mattered. All that mattered was that she was content. No ties, no commitments to anyone but herself. Well, other than the mountain rescue team and the occasional lost climber.

She didn't need anything else. She'd learned from the best—never look back. Not once had her father ever attempted to explain his sudden disappearance or his long absences. He simply showed up and pretended that all was as it should be.

"What about your folks?"

Heath's question snapped her back to attention. She had to stop zoning out like that.

"My…" She started to tell him that her mother was dead and that her father visited occasionally but she caught herself in time. She blinked, taken aback that she would stumble so badly with this man. Bolstering her defenses, she dished out the standard story, "There's no one but me." She produced the requisite sad smile. "Well, no one besides Rafe and my friends here."

He spotted the lie as soon as it was out of her mouth. She didn't miss the detection in his eyes before he disguised his surprise at her response. That unsettled her just a little. What did her family, or lack thereof, have to do with anything? Why would it matter if she chose not to talk about her family?

Beware of any strangers who come into your life.

Maybe she should heed her father's warning. Heath Murphy was the only stranger who had come into her life, other than tourists, in a very long time. His sudden appearance just prior to her father's warning might not be coincidence.

"I'm sorry to hear that," Heath said with a kind of sincerity that couldn't be faked, giving her something to puzzle over. "It's tough losing the people you care about."

He spoke from personal experience; she heard an old, lingering hurt in his words. But even bad guys had loved ones. However sincere he appeared, that didn't mean she could trust him. No one knew that better than her.

"Well, you know—" she pushed to her feet "—that's life." She picked up her plate and glass. "Good night, Mr. Murphy."

Rafe didn't like anyone dirtying up his sink once the kitchen was clean. Jayne quickly dumped the remains of her sandwich into the trash and deposited her dinnerware into the empty dishwasher. If Mr. Murphy was smart he'd do the same. Or maybe he wouldn't and Rafe would kick him out.

She could hope. Turning from the sink she came face-to-face with the man who had an uncanny ability to completely disorient her. At first she'd thought he'd decided to follow her example and clean up after himself, but instead he set his dishes on the counter next to her. Her gaze followed the movement, slid up those powerful arms and rested on that awesome chest. She hated herself for the weakness but she was only human.

"Look, I apologize if I brought up a tender subject when I asked about your family," he offered quietly. "I've got a few of my own. I can assure you I didn't intend to make you uncomfortable."

Jayne took a deep breath and gave her head a little shake. "Look, Murphy, why don't I just tell you the truth, okay?" Her heart started to pound when her brain caught up with her mouth. She'd always preferred honesty. Never had learned to hold her tongue the way she should. But this startled even her. "I don't know you," she stated bluntly, knowing full well it was too late to turn back now. "I don't trust you. And I have no intention of sleeping with you."

The last statement sent heat flooding to her cheeks and utter humiliation racing through the rest of her body. She could have left out that part. Dammit.

Instead of saying anything he took his time loading his dishes into the dishwasher, still blocking her escape with his body and giving her more than adequate time to grow utterly flustered. Cutting him some slack, she had just said a mouthful. Maybe he needed a moment to come up with a rebuttal.

Finally, after what felt like forever with him bending and reaching and making her feel more restless by the moment, he straightened and looked directly at her. She swallowed tightly and suddenly wished she had left the room at good-night.

"I'm sorry my presence disturbs you." His voice was soft, his expression concerned. "I'll try not to overstep my bounds again."

"I would appreciate that," she admitted, relieved to have the tension broken.

He shrugged, the movement drawing her attention like a fly to honey. "As for the sleeping together thing, I can't say I hadn't thought about that myself." He paused just long enough for the words to send a bolt of heat scorching through her. "But I would never compromise my principles. Good night, Ms. Stephens."

He walked out.

Her mouth dropped open in disbelief.

She was supposed to be the one to walk out. To have had the last word, the final warning.

Instead, he'd left her there feeling like a total idiot.

Not to mention she'd same as confessed that she'd thought about sleeping with him.

Uncertainty trembled through her. But she didn't want to sleep with him. Clearly he didn't want to sleep with her. What the hell had she been thinking admitting that to him? Temporary insanity! She'd lost it. Well, he'd certainly put her in her place.

A new blast of fury set off a minefield of outrage. Oh, he would regret that arrogant rebuke. Whether he'd intended to insult her or not, she would make him earn every word of this story the hard way. If he wanted to know what it was like to be a member of the mountain rescue team, she'd show him up close and personal.

Heath Murphy would rue the day he showed up in her town.

Chapter Six

Heath poured himself a second cup of Rafe's famous wake-the-dead coffee and resumed his position at a table a few feet away from Jayne and the mountain rescue team members gathered for a weekly breakfast meeting.

She hadn't spoken to him this morning. Rafe had banged on his door at 5:00 a.m. and passed along the info about the meeting. Jayne had either forgotten or chosen not to tell him since this was a regularly scheduled event. Considering her father's warning, he was prepared to work harder at earning her trust. Her oversight hadn't slowed down his reaction since he'd been awake already. The motion detectors already installed in her room warned him whenever she moved through any interior doors as well as the one exterior door that led into the upstairs corridor.

The meeting had started at six o'clock sharp. In the past hour they'd covered upcoming training sessions as well as traded humorous tourist stories. It had been the same in Heath's hometown. The locals couldn't help getting a laugh now and then at some of the overen-thusiastic tourists who showed up determined to portray themselves as professional skiers, snowboarders, hikers or climbers. Only when they broke a leg or got lost in the wilderness did they admit to their true amateur status.

Aspen was considerably larger and more popular than where Heath had grown up. Tucked away in the picturesque Roaring Fork Valley at the base of a towering mountain, Aspen had it all from what he'd seen so far: an abundance of shops ranging from gourmet restaurants to bars and pubs, from discount five-and-dimes loaded with tourist memorabilia to ritzy art galleries visited by the rich and famous—most within easy walking distance to the best hotels and resorts. The nightlife ranged from glitzy and glamorous to raw and untamed.

In his opinion Aspen was where the beautiful people came to ski and be seen in an extreme wilderness setting that, despite the haute couture, had managed to maintain its natural raw edges. But none of that meant anything to Heath. In fact, he used every ounce of determination he possessed to block out the insignificant details of the scene around him and to focus only on his mission. He didn't want to *experience* this environment.

He had to be here but he didn't have to soak it up.

So far, with the avalanche advisories still in place, he'd been able to avoid entirely *outdoor recreation.*

"So, we'll meet at the cabin at six tonight to do a gear check."

Heads around the table nodded.

Heath was surprised by that. Tomorrow was Jayne's birthday. He'd expected some sort of party or get-together in her honor. Maybe that was the purpose of tonight's meeting. If so, no one had let him in on the secret.

The mountain rescue cabin was located on the west end of Aspen's Main Street. The team's extra gear, topographic maps, communications system and most anything else they needed to perform rescues would be housed here. Though the team operated under the auspices of the Pitkin County Sheriff's department, Walt Messina pretty much ran things the way he wanted to, it seemed, without any flak. Jayne was second in command in spite of being female and younger than most of the other members. No one appeared to resent her position. A couple of other women were affiliated with the team but worked in a support capacity only.

It took guts and strength, physical as well as mental, to do what these folks did. Heath had worked, in his capacity as a member of law enforcement, with a mountain rescue team once. A long time ago…before the accident. As an experienced climber he'd fit right in with the other adrenaline junkies, but at least those guys had had a cause.

Heath's gut twisted with remembered dread and regret and he had to look away. He'd had no cause other than utter self-indulgence. Climbing had been a hazardous hobby, an ego pump. He'd sworn he would never be a part of anything like that again. And here he was, playing along, as if he hadn't failed…as if he hadn't let someone die.

His gaze moved back to rest on Jayne.

He could handle this. His teeth clenched to hold back the instant denial. Holding the uncertainty at bay had been fairly easy until now. This meeting, seeing this team together and listening to them discuss rescues, hit him a lot harder than he'd anticipated. But he would get past it. There was no way around it. His assignment depended upon his ability to fit in with this group.

"I got the latest word on the avalanche advisory first thing this morning," Walt said, drawing Heath's attention back to the conversation around the table. "If the weather cooperates today and tonight as forecasted the advisory will be lifted tomorrow."

A dagger of ice cut through Heath. That would mean all hiking and climbing operations would be back in business. Not everyone closed up shop for an advisory of this magnitude but some did, Happy Trails being one of them. Jayne would go back to her day job, leading visiting nature and thrill seekers through valleys and over peaks. And it was Heath's job to stay right on her heels, to keep watch for the target's appearance. The bitter dread that had coagulated in his gut evolved into heart-pumping fear. A line of sweat beaded on his brow.

He could do this. He knew the drill, had all the right experience.

But after over three years had he lost the feel? Should he be up front with Jayne and avoid the risk altogether?

"I'd like to run a hut check," Jayne announced, jarring Heath back from his troubling thoughts.

Walt frowned. "The hut associations are responsible

for spot checks. They rent them out. They do the maintenance."

"I know," Jayne returned, "but you said there had been a couple of break-ins reported. Supplies stolen. It wouldn't hurt for me to take a look, make sure all is as it should be before the advisory is lifted." She shrugged. "Even if the association does the same a second set of eyes can't hurt. I'm sure the sheriff's office would be interested in any additional detail I might pick up on."

Walt mulled over her suggestion just long enough to finish cranking Heath's tension to the breaking point. If the huts she spoke of were anything like the ones he'd encountered before, the small structures would be at higher elevations, nine or ten thousand feet at least. The huts were generally equipped with bunks, wood-burning or propane stoves and heaters and other basic supplies for survival during backcountry trips. Associations, owners rented them out for use during cross-country hauls for those who didn't care for sleeping on the snow-covered ground. Not to mention that anytime a climber or skier got into trouble, if he could make it to the nearest hut, his chances of survival until help arrived were greatly increased.

"Sounds like you've got cabin fever," Walt suggested with an I've-got-your-number grin. "Hut check if you want, just be careful out there and watch out for any of those snow shelves that might be about to deliver. Might be better if you took someone with you if you're going today."

"I'll do that," she assured her friend and boss. She

jerked her head in Heath's direction. "Mr. Murphy over there wants to see firsthand what my life is like, I thought I'd give him a little preview. That competence test I mentioned."

Curious gazes shifted in his direction. He managed a negligible nod to Walt and the others before his gaze collided with Jayne's and the blatant challenge there. This was payback. He wasn't quite sure for what just yet, but he could read the triumph in her eyes.

"You sure he's up to the physical requirements?" Paul Rice, an EMT, wanted to know.

Her gaze never deviated from Heath's as she provided a confident response. "He can handle it." She laughed and glanced around at her teammates. "If not I'll drag him out. In any case, he'll get his story, right? Without getting in the way of a real rescue."

Laughter tittered around the group but Heath didn't find her smart-ass remark funny at all. Giving her grace, she had no way of knowing the impact of what she'd suggested and if he survived the trip he'd make sure she never found out. Knowledge was power and he had to make sure she didn't outmaneuver him when things got dirty.

He had to stay in control of this asset, which equated to one thing: all the best cards had to be in his hand.

JAYNE WATCHED HEATH with a critical eye as he readied for the trek to the Alpine Hut on one of her favorite peaks. She knew the trail well, could basically make the journey with her eyes closed, so she wasn't worried. The snow cornices along her chosen path weren't nearly as worrisome as in some of the more traveled areas. If you stayed in the business long enough around here, you figured out the best routes or made some of your own. They'd check out this one hut and head back. Walt was right on that score. The huts were well maintained. But it had been as good an excuse as any to put her journalist shadow here in the hot seat.

Heath's efficiency at the task of prepping for the cold surprised her. She didn't have to give him the first instruction. He abided by one law any climber worth his salt did, always wear synthetics, absolutely no cotton. Cotton didn't repel water. He even picked the best brands when it came to outerwear, including gloves and snowshoes. Maybe he just had good instincts, but her own instincts were humming a different tune.

This guy had done this before.

Her gaze narrowed with suspicion. He'd certainly left out that pertinent detail of his background. Not that she'd asked that many questions, but one would think that when in Aspen following around a mountain rescue team member a guy would mention winter hiking and/or climbing experience.

"I'm ready," he announced when he'd pulled on the new parka that looked nothing like the elegant leather coat he'd had on when he arrived on her doorstep.

Very interesting turn of events.

"Let's do this, then."

Jayne clipped her pager at her waist and led the way

to her four-wheel-drive clunker. She should have washed it at some point during her downtime but then, what was the point? It would only get dirty again. Snow might look good on the mountains and in the yards of the lovely homes around town, but it turned ugly and muddy on the streets and side roads. They never showed that part in movies, she'd noticed.

Neither of them spoke as she drove along Highway 82 until they reached the turnoff that would lead to the trailhead. The county road had been plowed recently, which made the going a hell of a lot easier. As she parked on the roadside, choosing to walk the rest of the way to their destination, the sun shone between the majestic peaks in the distance. It was going to be a beautiful day and yet the tension continued to thicken between her and her companion.

Jayne had the sudden uneasy feeling that she'd made a mistake. She covertly studied Heath Murphy, wishing she could read his mind. Why would an investigative journalist come here to do a story on the life of a trail guide and mountain rescue team member if he didn't care for the subject? Or apparently felt uncomfortable with some aspect of it? It didn't make sense.

Besides, she couldn't see this guy being afraid of anything. He was strong, confident, even a little arrogant at times. She shouldered into her emergency pack and considered again how he'd seemed to know just the right items to buy for his own pack. A real paradox, this guy.

With the pack and other necessary accessories

draped on his back he looked even bigger and she was no petite gal. She stood five-seven, but he had to be six-two or -three. He weighed, she estimated, a hundred eighty pounds, most of which looked to be muscle if his chest and shoulders were any indication. Add to that a face with angles and planes that the sexiest man of the year would be jealous of and you had a hell of a great-looking guy. Even his nose was the perfect cut for balancing that classic square jaw.

Her gaze drifted down to his left hand. Why wasn't he married? Why didn't he get phone calls from a girlfriend? Of course, she supposed he could get all kinds of calls at night, but she hadn't heard his cell phone ring once and she hadn't noticed him making any calls.

Definitely strange.

Maybe he was a loner, she considered as she bent down and strapped on her snowshoes. He did the same. Again, his proficiency at pulling on and securing those time- and energy-saving accessories surprised her.

He looked upward abruptly, his fingers stilling in their work, his gaze colliding with hers.

"Something wrong?" he asked, his tone telling her he'd been aware that she was staring at him for some time now.

"Actually—" she dragged out the word long enough to recover her mental balance "—I was wondering if you'd done this before. You seem to know the routine though I kind of got the distinct impression you weren't looking forward to floundering around in the snow."

He straightened, smoothly shifting his gaze to the

rustic beauty ahead of them, all around them really. "I'm no virgin," he deadpanned, his attention moving back to her, "but it's been a really long time."

"Should I be concerned?" She had to ask though part of her wanted him to suffer, especially after that smart-alecky comment. God, where had that come from? She wasn't usually so heartless. But he made her angry…or something. Still, she couldn't let her annoyance at him get in the way of safety.

"I'll be fine."

His expression closed like steel doors slamming on a vault and she knew that the discussion was over.

Towering firs dotted the white landscape, their branches loaded with day-old snow. With several feet of compacted snow covering the plant life, the going should have been easier, but the fresh layer of fine powder made trail-breaking necessary. Every step she took sank in a foot or so—even with state-of-the-art snowshoes—ensuring maximum physical effort was involved.

To keep her mind off her companion, she mulled over the idea that tomorrow was her birthday and so far no one had mentioned a party. No one had mentioned her birthday at all. Her father hadn't even said anything. The possibility that maybe no one remembered that her birthday was less than twenty-four hours away only served to drive home the loneliness that gnawed at her from time to time. Usually she didn't let her lack of real family bother her. After all, she had Rafe and the guys.

But it wasn't the same. There were times when she had to admit that painful fact.

Admitting it and dwelling on it were very different animals and she refused to dwell on things she couldn't change. She forged forward, making a path in the deep, loose snow. Family was overrated anyway.

It was cold—around twenty degrees. But it didn't take long to warm up. Jayne paid close attention to her instincts. Even an experienced guide lost the trail from time to time. Definitely something she wanted to avoid. Losing the trail meant possibly going through deadfall from the surrounding firs and possibly crossing gullies shielded by the snow cover. There could be numerous other trip hazards hidden beneath the blanket of pristine white. Definitely something to avoid.

The farther they climbed the stiller the air became. The lack of breeze gave the peaceful environment a kind of surreal quality. The quiet was broken only by the breath that steamed in and out of their lungs. Heath hadn't lied about one thing—it had definitely been a while since he had done this. Though he'd stayed close on her heels when she took her early morning runs, this was an entirely different kind of workout. They had been moving at a good pace up this sharp ridge. She considered slowing down but knew they'd never make it to the hut and back before dark if she did.

"You okay back there?" She glanced back at him for the first time in almost an hour.

"Great," he insisted with a nod of his head.

But he didn't look great. Physically he appeared fine.

Tough as the fresh powder made it, this wasn't the kind of climb that would endanger anyone who was in good physical condition and he met that qualification hands down. Not to mention she was the one doing the trail-breaking, all he had to do was follow in her compacted footsteps.

No, it wasn't his outward appearance that gave her pause; it was something in his eyes. A dullness she hadn't seen before. That jarred her.

"We'll keep going then." Her instincts warring, she turned back to the trail and pushed forward. A couple more hours, tops, and they'd reach the false summit where the Alpine Hut stood. They'd replenish their fluids, eat, take a short break and then head back down.

Piece of cake.

HE WASN'T GOING TO make it.

By the time the hut came into view, after three and one half hours of steady climbing, Heath knew with dead certainty that he should have told her the truth up front.

Snowshoes and ski poles lashed to her pack, Jayne hustled up to the small, rustic cabin and unlocked the door. Heath made the final few steps a bit more slowly. He was in no hurry for her visual examination to confirm what she had clearly suspected two hours ago.

He was in real trouble here.

Panic had broken out in a cold, clammy sweat all over his body, in spite of, or maybe because of, the layers of synthetics he wore. Pants, shirt, parka, all of it was too familiar. Even the smell of the new fabric made his stomach churn. His heart pounded but it was more than the rigor of ascending several thousand feet…it was the whole package.

The vast whiteness. The mountains jutting toward the sky. The occasional scrub brush and spot of ground that defied the snow by remaining visible after a bona fide blizzard. He had tried to talk himself down from the anxiety. Blamed the physical symptoms on the altitude and the fact that he hadn't climbed in more than three years.

But it was none of those things.

It was the memories.

The way she'd looked at him before she'd fallen…before he'd failed her.

His fault.

He'd dragged her to Utah, insisted that there was this one peak he just had to climb. He wanted her there with him. She'd relented, though climbing was far from her favorite leisure time activity.

Only one of them had climbed back down that mountain.

It had taken days to recover her body.

No one had blamed him. It was an accident.

But he knew then and he knew now that it was his fault. She only went to please him.

Heath stalled just inside the door of the cabin, tore off his pack, gloves and parka and started to pace the small main room. But the anxiety only escalated. Being inside…this place… It made things worse. The smell of something burning jerked his attention across the room.

Jayne had built a fire.

He blinked, tried to steady himself. She already suspected something wasn't right. He had to get back in control of the situation. He'd known this would happen. No one else at the Colby Agency had possessed his climbing skills. His selection had been necessary. There had been no time to prepare another investigator for this assignment. Not to mention the I.A. investigation had dictated that he be the one. He'd thought that maybe he could handle it. But he'd been wrong.

A new realization made Heath go stone cold. Right now, at this precise moment, she was not safe with him. He wasn't at all sure he could protect her if the need arose. He hoped like hell Howard Stephens didn't choose this particular moment to show up. He'd managed to keep his guard up fairly well on the way up, surveying the area, watching for any sign of movement, though he doubted if he'd been at his best.

Heath's eyes closed and for the first time since the morning began he let the climate's bitter cold invade his senses. He was freezing. His fingers were numb in spite of the high-tech gloves he'd worn. His leg muscles ached and he felt more exhausted than—

"Okay, enough of this."

Jayne's firm tone ushered his eyes open. She stared at him as if she feared he might make a run for it any second. And, truthfully, that's exactly how he felt, as if he needed to run all the way back down this damned mountain and not look back. He clenched his fists, set his jaw hard. Anything to keep himself from flying apart.

Deep in his gut he'd known this was a bad idea. But not once had he considered that it would be quite this bad. He'd thought he had put the past behind him. He'd been wrong.

"What's going on?" Jayne demanded, drawing his attention back to the here and now. "You look terrified. What the hell are you doing following me around, Murphy, if you're scared of heights?"

"I'm not afraid of heights," he growled, too frustrated to keep the savage sound out of his tone.

She glanced at the pack, parka and gloves he'd discarded so carelessly. Whatever she thought of that she kept to herself. Instead of pounding him with more questions, she pulled the food from her own pack as well as his and warmed it over the flames. He stood back, unable to participate, and watched her methodical, familiar movements. His mind immediately conjured flashes of memory of him doing that very thing. He'd been there…done that…one time too many already. He had to be insane to be here now.

The room started to heat up and Heath unbuttoned the Gore-Tex shirt he wore over two layers of full-length underclothes. The floor glistened with the snow that had melted from their boots. He wet his lips and swallowed back another surge of panic. Control, he had to grab back control. They were safe. There was no need to panic. And, yet, he couldn't slow the adrenaline soaring through his veins.

He curled and uncurled his fingers and looked around the room for something to focus on or something to do.

"The woodpile looks a little low," he muttered, more to himself than to the only other human being within a few thousand feet of him.

She set the grub on the table and looked from him to the woodpile in the corner and back. "There's probably more out back. I'll bring some in to replace what we use after we eat. *You* need to eat and calm down."

He shook his head and reached for his parka and gloves. "I'll take care of the wood."

Before Jayne could say more he'd tramped out the door. What the hell was the deal here?

She went to the window, forgetting the food that would get cold a hell of a lot faster than it had gotten warm, and watched as he checked a couple of snowdrifts before he found the woodpile. He gathered an armful of chopped wood and hauled it into the hut.

When he'd stacked it in the corner he turned back to her. "That's the last of what's been prepared for the stove." He gestured to the wood-burning stove she had going at maximum capacity. "If there's an ax around here I'll chop some more."

He couldn't be serious. "Of course there's an ax in the hall storage closet, but you don't need to do that. The owner or the renters take care of that, it's—"

He cut her off, those dark brown eyes going from a

listless deadness to a glittering granite glare. "It's like you said, it doesn't hurt to make sure all is as it should be before the avalanche advisory is lifted."

Well, he had her there. Before she could even attempt to argue with her own words, he'd stormed back out into the frigid air.

Not so foolish as to ignore her own needs, Jayne nibbled at her food as she observed his maniac episode and that's all she knew to call it. He'd exposed a pile of larger sticks of wood and was now hefting the ax to chop them into smaller, stove-size pieces. It was insane. Though she doubted she had to worry about him freezing to death. It just wasn't right.

After thirty minutes of grueling labor, including stacking the newly chopped wood into a neat pile, he came inside again. This time he stomped most of the snow off his boots first. He put the ax away and came back into the main room where she stood, flabbergasted.

"Anything else you'd like to do around here?" She waved her arms in punctuation of the question. "I don't know, maybe like clear the snow off the roof?"

He didn't answer, just grabbed up his cold food and ravenously devoured it.

When he'd finished fueling his body and cleaned up the remains her patience slipped again. "Okay, Murphy, let's have it," she demanded, hands planted on her Gore-Tex–clad hips. There was nothing attractive about cold weather gear for climbers. The thick layers of protective clothing probably made her hips several inches wider.

She shook herself and refused to even speculate on why that thought had never once occurred to her before. This *thing* going on between her and him was too bizarre. They were strangers. She didn't even like him. Especially right now.

"Have what?" He avoided her eyes, pretending to be concerned with something outside the front window.

"You're not fooling me for a second." She marched up to him and poked him in the chest, not that the move did much good with all those heavy clothes in the way. But it did get his attention. "I know a panic attack when I see one. I've dealt with plenty when overzealous climbers underestimate their fears. You almost lost it on the way up here. Why?"

They didn't have time for this. The daylight was wasting away while she played twenty questions with a virtual stranger. She had to be losing it, too. But there was something in his eyes…an emotion that compelled her to ask…to understand. Every instinct told her that this man was far too strong and capable to be turned inside out by a moderate climb. There was more…a lot more.

His answer was so long in coming she'd wondered if he intended to answer at all. Finally he did, but not before wiping his face and eyes clean of emotion. "I told you I'd done this a few times before."

She nodded once, afraid to speak or make any sudden moves for fear of stopping him.

One shoulder jerked in what was likely intended as a shrug. "There was an accident." His gaze connected with hers on a level that took her breath. She could feel his agony. "I don't want to talk about it." She blinked, he didn't. "I haven't climbed since."

She wanted to curl up and die. What a jerk she'd been.

"I'm sorry." She let go a heavy breath. "I shouldn't have dragged you up here like this." He didn't respond, just stared at her. "But I wanted to get back at you for…" Man, her motivation sounded so lame now. But she owed him the truth. "You walked out on me last night and I was supposed to walk out on you," she said in a rush.

He didn't look completely surprised at her silly admission, but then he didn't look happy about it either.

He blew out a weary breath of his own and shoved his hands into the pockets of his cold-weather pants. "Well, if it makes you feel any better," he offered, those dark eyes soft and sexy as hell once more, "it wasn't easy."

A moment of awkward silence hung in the air. Jayne wasn't sure whether she should demand to know what his statement meant or run for her life.

She decided on the latter.

"We should go. Walt was right, this was totally unnecessary."

She didn't give him an opportunity to debate the assessment. She put out the fire she'd built, carried out the ash and locked up the hut, safe and sound.

Just under four hours later they were back at the trailhead and climbing into her old clunker. She drove straight to town as quickly as the slick road allowed, parked and immediately headed up to her apartment.

All without exchanging a word or glance with Heath Murphy.

Chapter Seven

Jayne soaked in the tub for nearly an hour. She'd had to keep adding hot water in an effort to ward off the chill that seemed to come from her very bones. It was scarcely six o'clock and already she felt like midnight had come and gone.

She kept seeing his eyes…the agony.

There was an accident.

I haven't climbed since.

She squeezed her lids shut and tried to banish the memory but it simply would not go away.

She opened her eyes and looked at her hands, the small calluses there. The physical rigor of her work left its mark other places as well. She lifted her left leg from the water and studied the jagged line on her calf where she'd taken her first fifty-yard tumble down into a gulley a few years ago. Twenty-eight stitches had been required to sew her up. Bruises and other aches and pains came with the territory on a regular basis.

But there were other marks, the kind that scarred a person's heart and soul. The ones like Heath bore. She moved her head slowly from side to side in confusion. She hadn't noticed when they first met. She should have. Anyone who'd ever watched someone fall to their death or who had dragged a body out of a river a few thousand feet below where the victim had fallen had a look about them. It wasn't pretty. She should know. She stared into that haunted expression every day in the mirror.

Her worst nightmares came from the rescues. Not the ones who survived but the ones who didn't. Those times when a rescue became a body recovery. Kids were the worst. God, she didn't know how parents dealt with the loss. Expert climbers fell occasionally. Not often, but once in a great while. She remembered one retrieval where a man with thirty years' climbing experience behind him disappeared. It had taken days to find him. He'd fallen but hadn't died immediately. Before beginning what would be his final journey he'd opted not to carry a transmitter, commonly known as an avalanche beacon. He had carried his cell phone. But the vicious cold got the battery and then it got him. He'd left a journal of sorts down to the bitter end. His last entry spoke of feeling splendidly warm.

The phenomena was kind of like a mirage in the desert, a person suffering from the final stages of hypothermia would feel incredibly warm and even start shedding the very garments keeping him alive.

An experience like that had left its mark on Heath. She'd known people who lost friends and relatives but it didn't keep them away from the challenge of climbing. It was like an addiction, got in your blood. You couldn't deny the rush. That's what kept people like her going back out there bringing back the lost even after scraping up body parts from rocky gullies.

But Heath hadn't gone back. Today had been tough on him. She'd watched him almost come apart right in front of her. Sheer determination had held him together enough to walk off that mountain. A new kind of respect for this man sprouted inside her. Mixed with that respect was guilt for putting him through the pain. But she hadn't known. She should have, but she hadn't. His courage had won out, though. He was every bit as strong mentally as he was physically.

The dreamy smile that pushed across her face fell just as quickly. But that didn't explain or excuse his final remark in that hut. *Well, if it makes you feel any better…it wasn't easy.*

What wasn't easy? Walking away? That didn't make sense…unless he was attracted to her and suffered the same malady of need as she did.

"Don't be ridiculous," she grumbled under her breath. He liked teasing her, that was clear. Definitely liked watching her, but that was part of the reporter gig, right? He couldn't do his job without getting to know her and observing her routine.

Oh well. She was probably better off not knowing what he'd meant. In a couple of days he would be gone anyway. She was pretty sure he was only hanging around in hopes of having the opportunity to observe an actual rescue.

A new line of confusion worried her brow. That didn't make sense. If he didn't climb anymore, how was he supposed to observe anything? She had a strong suspicion she wasn't supposed to have seen what she saw today. Just how the heck had he expected to get through the ordeal anyway? He'd be a liability. He had to know that.

She sighed and relaxed more deeply into the water. She was too tired to figure this out. But there was definitely something out of sync here. If he hadn't come to write about a rescue, then why here, why her?

Her father's warning exploded inside her brain, evaporating the oxygen in her lungs.

Killers didn't have panic attacks, she reasoned. This guy had a full-fledged anxiety episode. She'd witnessed it with her own eyes. Spies and assassins didn't succumb to mere human frailties…did they?

"Just give it up, girl," she muttered as she reluctantly dragged herself from the water. A few more minutes and she'd be a prune. Tomorrow was her birthday. She wanted to look good even if no one noticed.

She wrapped a towel around her hair and then another around her body. She'd eat in tonight. Didn't feel like company and there would be a crowd in the bar. The outdoor enthusiasts would be in full swing, celebrating the lifting of the avalanche advisory.

That scene would just have to happen without her. She had a bottle of wine somewhere in her tiny kitchen, cheese, crackers. Hey, sounded like a party to her.

She stared at her reflection in the mirror. She'd be

twenty-five in a few hours. No boyfriend. Not even any prospects. That was truly sad.

And then an old, too-familiar companion crept in.

Loneliness.

HEATH WALKED THE perimeter once more before going back inside. He glanced at the display on his phone occasionally, quickly looking away when he noted Jayne's exact position. He drew in a deep breath of cold air. For the last hour she'd been in the tub. He'd known he couldn't hang around his room and *not* look at that monitor.

No problem. He needed to check the area anyway. Uneasiness nagged at him. He'd accessed the system with his cell phone, picking up the monitor's feed. The image was small enough to lack detail but sufficient to set him at ease as to her every move.

He stopped and turned around. The sidewalk wasn't crowded just yet. In another hour the streets would be jam-packed, but for now, it was pretty deserted. But the hair standing on the back of his neck warned him that he wasn't the only one watching the Altitude Bar and Grill.

He was here.

Not just in the area, but *here*.

Heath surveyed the street, then the building before him. Its one-hundred-year-old facade was right in keeping with the old mining-town look still present around Aspen, as was the rustic interior. Even he couldn't deny that this was a lovely town. Picturesque most certainly. The snow-covered roofs and streets lit with holiday lights made the new as well as the old look cozy and welcoming. But it was the snow-capped peaks in the distance that drew folks from all around the country.

Not the kind of place one would generally expect to find a man like Howard Stephens lurking. But he was here all the same. Heath could feel the anticipation building and this time it had nothing to do with altitude.

He glanced right once more then headed toward the entrance of the bar. He'd lost a lot of ground today. Had allowed Jayne to see his weakness. She would have questions. Those questions would lead to more questions. Soon she would realize that two and two, in this case, did not equal four. And then the situation would spiral completely out of control.

Somehow he had to stop that from happening.

He hesitated at the door. His old psychologist would say that he'd faced his demons today. And he had. But he wasn't sure the challenge had accomplished anything other than distracting and exposing him.

He'd been distracted when they arrived back into town this evening but not so much so as not to notice the change. His old, reliable cop instincts had surfaced in the nick of time. He'd felt someone watching Jayne, watching him, as they'd exited her vehicle and headed into the bar. With each passing second since, that well-honed instinct he'd depended upon more than once had been sending him a warning with escalating urgency.

Jayne might not have the opportunity to figure out

who he really was and why he was here. He had a bad feeling that learning who and what her father was might just take precedence sooner than he'd hoped.

One good thing had come of today's loss of control. Jayne had connected with him on at least one level. Even if she only felt sorry for him, it was a starting point. He'd need all the help he could get before this was over.

He checked the screen on his cell phone once more before going inside. Jayne was busily drying her hair, still clad in that damned towel. His throat went instantly and fiercely dry. This was the first time since…in a long time that he'd wanted a woman the way he wanted Jayne. He respected her, was awed by her determination. Maybe it was that she so effortlessly achieved what he'd once loved. To stand on some fourteen-thousand-foot summit and peer out over the world had once completed something inside him. That, he realized then, might just be the unexplainable connection he shared with her.

She moved with nature, not against it. He felt reasonably sure that watching her was all that had prevented today from turning out far worse. She'd kept him grounded to a degree.

Needing her, however, would be a liability for both of them in the end.

"Hey, Murphy! Come over here!"

Rafe gestured wildly for Heath to join him at the end of the bar. A small crowd had already gathered around the tables and the music whined and coiled its way around the room.

"What's up?" He paused at the bar, anxious to get to his room...to a better, larger image of the woman upstairs. He groaned inwardly at his inability to keep his head on straight. Oh, hell, what was one more admission today?

"Listen, Murphy," Rafe said in a stage whisper, "you gotta help me out here."

"Rafe, I don't—"

"There isn't much time, you've got to take care of this for me," the old man insisted.

Heath held up his hands in the classic surrender gesture. "Tell me what you need me to do."

Rafe edged closer as if his instructions were top secret. "Go upstairs and keep my girl occupied until I tell you to bring 'er down."

A frown furrowed a path across Heath's brow. "How's that?" The music was loud, maybe he'd misunderstood.

"It's her birthday, man," Rafe urged. "Keep her busy until I get everything in order down here."

Heath surveyed the crowd more closely and recognized the other mountain rescue team members and several people he'd noted Jayne chatting with when she'd waited tables.

"Look back here." Rafe grabbed him by the arm and hauled him to the kitchen door. He grinned like a new grandfather when he pointed out the enormous cake holding a place of honor on the island.

"I see." Heath nodded. "I'll go up now." His entire body tightened at the prospect. Rafe had no way of knowing that sending him to her room was not a good idea.

"Give me the number of that slick cell phone you carry," Rafe said, grabbing a napkin and the pen from his shirt pocket.

Heath rattled off the number and headed toward the back stairs. He hesitated at the short corridor that led past the public rest rooms long enough to give the old guy a two-fingered salute. Rafe grinned and rubbed his hands together in anticipation.

At the end of the corridor was a door marked "Employees Only" that led to the storeroom where the stairs were located. A smile tugged at Heath's lips as he double-timed it up the ancient steps. He should have known her friends wouldn't let her down. He was glad. He'd seen her eyes after that call from her father. As contented as Jayne liked to pretend she was, she was lonely. She would love this.

He stood outside her door for several seconds before he knocked. His hesitation wasn't about courage, it was about that other "c" word. He was having a hell of a time with control where she was concerned. Where this whole case was concerned. She'd likely figured out that walking away from her without doing something stupid like kissing her last night was what he'd meant about it not being easy.

Just another admission he should have kept to himself. Already regret weighed heavily on his shoulders. He didn't want to be the one to do this to her...to show her the truth.

Her door opened and she stood there, now wearing that ragged terry cloth robe and still clutching a hairbrush. She blinked away the surprise at seeing him and asked, "What's up?"

Whether she'd intended the next move or not, he couldn't say, but the one thing he could predict was its effect. Her gaze slid down his body, from the V neck of the lightweight sweater he wore beneath the jacket that concealed his shoulder holster and weapon to the well-worn jeans he preferred over any other trousers. Muscles already taut with tension turned rock hard with want.

Definitely a bad sign of how this day could ultimately end.

"Can I come in?" he asked, drawing her gaze out of dangerous territory and back to his face.

Big mistake.

That wide-eyed innocent stare glowed with desire. She blinked. "Sure."

He waited for her to step back and open the door wider. Keeping physical distance was imperative right now if he was to have any hope whatsoever of keeping this on a professional level. In his wildest dreams he would never have imagined it would be this difficult. The concept that he might not be cut out for this kind of work nudged him for the second time since he had left Chicago.

He'd done a little undercover work back in his cop days, but he'd never had this much trouble keeping perspective.

"Is something wrong?" she asked, eyeing him speculatively. Not that he could blame her, he'd pretty much lost it on that mountain today. She had good reason to doubt his sanity.

He tried not to look at the shoulder bared by the loose fitting robe when she inclined her head to the right like that. "Ah…maybe you'd be more comfortable if you got dressed. I don't mind waiting." He gestured to the closest chair. "I'd like to get some more background information. If that's okay?" The house of lies he was building felt shakier with each one he added.

Confusion skittered across her makeup-free face. "Okay. Good." She shrugged, which bared more of that gorgeous shoulder. "I'll…ah…get dressed."

When she'd left the room Heath breathed a little easier. He took advantage of the moment and looked around to see if anything had changed since he was here before. He wondered if her father had come into the room. He'd had the perfect opportunity while they were climbing today. Heath slipped a palm-size electronics detector from his jacket pocket and scanned the room and the tiny, adjoining kitchen nook. The only bugs he found were the ones Cole's people had installed, but that left the bedroom and bathroom. That opportunity might not present itself unless he could slip away from the party for a few moments tonight.

Heath paused to study a framed photograph of a much-younger Jayne and another woman who he suspected was her mother. The resemblance was there, too dramatic not to notice. He hadn't found any pictures of her father, didn't see any now. Stephens had probably warned her not to keep any around, a sacrifice of the job. Jayne was a smart lady; he wondered if she blindly accepted his explanations for his long absences and stealthy behavior. It seemed unlikely to Heath, but then a kid would do most anything for a parent's approval.

He thought of his own parents and how he rarely got down to see them anymore. He'd blamed his negligence on the accident, like he did everything else, but maybe it was more related to the idea that he didn't want to see the accusation in their eyes. Or, like his psychologist had suggested, maybe it was merely his own self-guilt that made him see and feel only what he expected to see. Either way, he couldn't deal with it.

"That's me and my mom when I turned eighteen," Jayne said from behind him. "Less than a year before she died."

Heath turned to face her. "You look a lot like her."

She smiled, her eyes distant with memories. "Thanks. We were very close."

"Staying in tonight?" he asked, changing the subject.

She looked down self-consciously at her attire, faded jeans and an equally fatigued Altitude T-shirt. He hadn't meant to make her feel self-conscious. It's just that he knew what was in store. He couldn't help grinning at those bare feet. Pink nail polish gleamed on her toes. Cute. Sexy as hell. Something else for him to think about when he should be concentrating on his job.

"Yeah." She shrugged. "I'm spending the night with a bottle of wine."

He'd noticed the bottle on the kitchen counter…and the single stemmed glass.

"It's my birthday," she explained as she padded over to the counter. "At least it will be in about four and a half hours." She uncorked the wine and reached for the glass. "Would you like to join me?"

The voice of reason told him to say no, but he just couldn't turn her down. She looked so vulnerable and needy. Where was the strong, determined young woman he'd first met some forty-eight hours ago? Apparently he wasn't the only one baring weaknesses today.

He took the glass from her. Their fingers brushed, the resulting sizzle chasing away the last of his good sense.

She prowled in the cupboard for another glass and came out with a plastic one sporting the logo of a local Mexican restaurant. That blush of self-consciousness tinted her cheeks again. "I don't have guests often," she explained.

"Here." He exchanged glasses with her. "It's your birthday."

The gesture brought another of those sweet smiles to her lips stealing Heath's ability to take a breath.

When she'd poured his wine he offered a toast, "To you, may this be the best birthday ever."

She touched her glass to his. "To me," she murmured before taking a sip of the amber liquid.

But this wouldn't be her best birthday ever. That's why he was here, to rip away the fantasy. To make her see the worst in the man whose shadow she'd clung to all these years.

Heath drank deeply in hopes of drowning the guilt, but it wouldn't work. He'd tried that before. That he'd gone into this with his eyes wide open only made him more of a monster and he had to live with that. Even if what he was about to do was for her own good.

Or was it?

Why couldn't Danes have found some other way to lure her father? Then the man would simply have stopped calling, stopped making those rare visits. She would never have had to know the truth. She could have made up a dozen different romantic and heroic scenarios for his disappearance.

Damn Cole Danes.

Heath clutched his drink so hard it was a miracle the plastic didn't crack.

"Murphy, I was wondering—"

"Heath," he interjected, his voice stilted. "You were going to call me Heath, remember?" She should at least be on a first-name basis with the man who was about to turn her world upside down.

"Heath," she relented. "I know you wanted to ask me some questions, but, if you're up to it, I'd like to talk about that accident you mentioned. What happened to you today…" She looked away for a moment. "I'd like to help."

To his supreme gratitude his cell phone rang just then. "Excuse me." He set his glass aside and turned away from her expectant expression to answer the call just in case it wasn't Rafe. "Murphy."

"We're ready down here," Rafe whispered.

"I understand." Heath closed the phone, scarcely suppressing the smile that tickled his lips. Rafe was something. He would be here for her. As would the others on her rescue team. They would help Jayne through the devastation to come. That assuaged his conscience a fraction, but it didn't relieve him of responsibility.

He dropped the phone back into his jacket pocket and faced the woman who seriously messed with his objectivity. "I have to pick up an incoming fax at the Mail Boxes Etc., across the street," he said without hesitation. "Would you walk over with me? We can talk on the way." That last comment was purposely misleading. He wouldn't be talking about the accident. Couldn't. But he needed her to go with him, for that she needed motivation. More lies. Funny thing was, each one pinged his conscience a little harder.

She glanced at the clock. "Are they still open?"

He shrugged, dismissing her concern. "Must be, they called."

She set her wineglass on the counter. "A walk would be good."

She grabbed her ever-present pager then tugged on her ankle boots and he helped her into her coat, relishing the feel of her hair against his hand. This was the first time she'd worn it down. He liked it that way. The image of the silky stuff gliding over his skin as they made love loomed large in his overactive imagination before he could stop it.

Another bad omen.

IT WAS A GOOD THING Jayne knew the stairs down to the ground floor by heart because she couldn't take her eyes off the man at her side.

The stark contrast between what she'd witnessed on that mountain and the man with her right now totally blew her away. So polished, so damned good-looking. Perfect composure, radiating strength and confidence.

Whatever had happened to him was too horrible to talk about. Too horrible to relive and yet he made that climb with her today as if his life had depended upon it.

The two extremes didn't mesh, made no sense at all. Why would he put himself through that kind of mental anguish to get a story? Did his job depend upon this one story? He'd said he worked for a number of publications. Maybe his career had taken a downward spiral and he hoped for *the* story that would put him back on top.

Whatever the case, she had to respect that kind of grit. She'd known he was strong from the beginning but that glimpse of vulnerability today had shaken her to the core. She'd never met a man confident enough in his masculinity to risk such a display.

God almighty, she was falling for this guy.

A soft sigh ached out of her. And he was only here temporarily.

How could this happen?

She'd sworn never to let this happen. Okay, it hadn't yet. At least not completely. Firming her resolve as they reached the door that led out into the corridor, she promised herself not to let this relationship progress any further into personal terrain. From now on this would be a purely professional relationship of interviewee and interviewer. Nothing more.

"Jayne." He stopped shy of opening the door.

She looked up at him and every speck of willpower she'd gathered scattered like snowflakes on a windy day. "Yes?"

If he hadn't looked at her that way, hadn't let his gaze drop to her lips, she might have had a chance, but he did look at her that way...as if he wanted to kiss her more than he'd ever wanted to do anything in his life.

"Happy birthday," he said softly. He kissed her cheek and her heart stumbled. In that infinitesimal moment before he drew away—that throbbing pause that turned one's knees to mush—he whispered two words that sent uncertainty rushing through her veins. "Forgive me."

She stared at his profile as he opened the door and ushered her into the corridor. Before she could demand an explanation hundreds of arms were reaching for her, voices crying out, "Happy birthday, Jayne!"

Her friends dragged her toward the center of the room, away from Heath, where a huge birthday cake awaited.

As Rafe draped an arm around her shoulders the entire crowd broke into a seriously pathetic rendition of the birthday song. Jayne couldn't help herself, she had to cry. Foolish tears rolled down her cheeks and the members of her team all had a good laugh.

"Well, now Jayne," Walt said, pushing his way to her other side, "we didn't mean to make you cry like a baby, but since we did, we'll need a picture for future corroboration."

Cameras flashed as she swiped her eyes and struggled not to laugh. This would ruin her tough-as-nails reputation. "Just wait," she threatened, "I know your birthdays, too." She looked from Walt to Rafe. "I'll make sure the funeral director's hearse is parked out front."

"Let's get this party started before the little lady gets to any of the rest of us," Chad, her team partner, suggested.

Cheers of approval went up as someone pumped up the music's volume. Chad gave her a hug, then Paul. She lost count of the number of people who wrapped their arms around her and pointed to gifts piled on one end of the bar. She hadn't even noticed the gifts.

She looked for Heath but couldn't find him in the crowd. Had he meant that she should forgive him for being in on this surprise? The words, his tone, felt too somber for something as happy as this.

Forget it. This was her birthday party and she could do anything she wanted, including letting her hair all the way down for the first time in a very long time.

HEATH KNEW STEPHENS was out here. His weapon palmed, he moved around the building once more, watching for any movement between the parked cars.

He'd seen someone at the bar's main entrance. He'd

gotten only a glimpse of the man's profile, but he was ninety-nine percent certain it was him.

Daddy had come to see his little girl on her birthday.

Fury pounding in his skull, Heath searched the entire parking lot, looked inside every car before accepting that the area was clear. He had to be sure Stephens was gone for now.

Heath clenched his jaw hard when he found no sign of the man. *Bastard.*

How could he do this to his own daughter?

Heath went back inside and quickly scanned the crowd to ensure all was as it should be.

Jayne's friends toasted her over and over and the many famous Altitude concoctions were loaded onto tray after tray, never allowing anyone to go thirsty. She'd shed her coat. The simple T-shirt clung to the soft swells and lean valleys of her torso. The jeans complimented her lower anatomy with every bit as much natural sensuality. She had an amazing body. His throat parched sending him in search of a bottle of water behind the bar. There'd be nothing else alcoholic for him tonight.

He kept his distance from Jayne for the remainder of the party. He wanted this night to be filled with good, with no significant memories of him. No one's birthday should be tainted with the kind of hurt his name would be forever associated with in her mind. She deserved better than that. Had already been let down, big-time, by the bastard who'd sired her.

And then there was that other bastard. The one

who'd sent Heath here, who'd used Jayne as nothing more than human bait to lure in her evil father.

Men like Cole Danes were barely a cut above the lowlifes they hunted down.

This—Heath's gaze followed Jayne across the dance floor in another man's arms—should never have happened.

But it was too late for regrets now.

The game had already started.

Chapter Eight

"I've had visual contact."

Heath had waited until dawn to contact Danes. He'd hoped his anger would have diminished to some extent by morning but it hadn't. His attention remained fixed on the monitor's image of a sleeping Jayne as he paced his small room. He wanted to reach across this telephone line and punch Danes for setting this stage.

"Excellent. I knew he would be close."

Heath held his breath in an effort to slow the avalanche of fury rushing through him, but the move was futile.

"Tell me why it had to be this way."

His words were bitter, cold, filled with animosity for the man in charge. He didn't need to spell it out. Danes would understand.

"It's the *only* way."

Heath shook his head, his fingers clutching the cell phone with white-knuckled intensity. "I won't accept that."

An unexpected silence followed.

When it dragged on Heath was suddenly certain he'd

crossed some unseen line with Danes. His new career might very well be over before it had much of a chance to get started…but he didn't care. This was wrong. He couldn't imagine Cole Danes having any kind of explanation that would make it right.

"The information that would clarify the situation for you is highly classified."

Heath rolled his eyes. "Screw that crap. I'm not buying it."

Another prolonged silence.

"Since this mission depends solely upon your complete focus and cooperation I'll make a judgment call and take the position that you *need* to know."

Anticipation surged, momentarily slowing Heath's mounting fury. "Don't yank my chain, Danes," he warned. He'd had enough of this guy's games. If he knew more about Stephens he should have told Heath up front. He didn't like going in blind on any level. He damned sure didn't want any half truths now.

"I will give you the justification your conscience needs," Danes allowed, "but know this, Mr. Murphy, I find insubordination on any level unacceptable."

Heath choked out a laugh. "If you think a threat is going to do the trick, Danes, you're sadly mistaken. I didn't sign on for these head games. You tell me why this is going down this way. Tell me now or I'll take charge of the situation myself."

"You mean," Danes suggested, "the way you took charge of the situation when your partner used your distraction to get away with murder?"

The words had the desired effect. The rug jerked right out from under Heath's feet.

"Or perhaps you mean the way you took charge of the situation when your girlfriend found herself on a slippery ledge and fell to her death."

"You son of a bitch." Heath slammed his cell phone closed. His fingers curled around it as if he could somehow prevent more of the truth from spilling out of it. He closed his eyes and shook with the effort of holding his emotions together. A part of him wanted to beat the hell out of Danes. But another part of him, the part that recognized the truth in the bastard's words, wanted to cry out with the agony that still lived in the furthest recesses of his brain. Never completely going away.

He'd left a vital piece of himself on that damned ledge three years ago and nothing was ever going to bring it back. He'd screwed up and she had paid. His inability to pull himself back together had allowed his new partner to hurt innocent people…and almost get away with it.

But, by God, he wouldn't screw up this time. Jayne's safety depended upon him. She might never forgive him for his part in all this, but he had to protect her.

Heath flipped open his phone and stabbed the necessary numbers. He didn't wait for a hello. "Tell me what you know," he demanded. He could imagine the look of satisfaction on Danes's face.

"Twenty years ago Howard Stephens was more or less a two-bit hood for hire. It's true he spent a couple of years on the military's payroll in a capacity much like a Central Intelligence asset under the curiously vague network of Special Forces shadow operations. But his value was greatly reduced when his superiors discovered his fetish for selling secrets."

"I'm not interested in ancient history, Danes. Save it for the textbooks."

A hum of amusement vibrated across the line. "Where is your patience, Mr. Murphy?"

Heath opted not to answer what he presumed to be a rhetorical question.

"Our Mr. Stephens joined forces with a man named Errol Leberman, the arch nemesis of James Colby."

James Colby was Victoria's first husband. Heath was aware that the Colby Agency had been plagued by an enemy named Leberman who was responsible for the kidnapping of Victoria's son, Jim Colby. But Jim was back now, after years of brutal persecution by Leberman.

"And you think Stephens is the one who kept the information flow between someone at the Colby Agency and Leberman," Heath finished for Danes. "I've heard all that before. And as sorry as I am for what happened to the Colby family, what does this have to do with Jayne Stephens? Why does she have to suffer for her father's sins?"

"Relax, Murphy, we're only now getting to the good part."

His condescending tone set Heath on edge all over again.

"Leberman was so preoccupied with revenge he

more or less allowed Stephens to do as he pleased with the little mercenary operation he'd started. A grievous error in judgment. Stephens decided that the occasional foray into third world countries to murder and steal weren't lucrative enough. So he started another kind of service right here in this country."

Dread twisted in Heath's gut.

"His team specialized in assassinating those most killers for hire preferred to avoid. Cops, members of the military, even the occasional politician, always making the murder look like an accident. A shoot-out with a drug dealer, a helicopter crash or simple car accident. Most of his clients are foreigners. Persons from countries who, shall we say, have a distaste for our way of life. Few things happen by accident, Murphy. A man like Stephens could, for example, perpetrate an uprising of Iraqi rebels against American peacekeeping troops and it would be blamed on the terrorists or the fallen regime. People believe what they want to. They need an explanation for why things happen. Men like Stephens prey upon that need. He has no conscience, is loyal only to himself."

The whirlwind of emotions Heath had tangled with all night gave way to astonishment. "Why hasn't someone stopped him before now?" He shook his head in disbelief.

"No one knew who he was until recently. You see, according to the military's records, Howard Stephens died eighteen years ago, about the same time the Colby child went missing."

That didn't make sense. "But he's kept in touch with his daughter."

"A daughter who protects him, does she not? What did she tell you about her father?"

A chill leeched into Heath's bones. *There's no one but me.*

"But he's made contact with her," Heath argued. "Has surfaced more than once?"

Danes hissed a breath of impatience. "No one knew to look for him. There was no reason. He was dead. He has operated under a number of aliases all these years. It was only discovered recently that he was still alive."

An epiphany struck Heath fast and furiously. "You found him," he said, almost to himself. He could see that. Cole Danes would find the truth when no one else could. He was relentless like that.

"Lucas Camp hired me to look into this case. I traced the connection to Stephens."

Heath felt stunned all over again. This was entirely too much to digest.

"We have to stop him, Murphy. He knows we've done what no one else ever could. We're on to him. And we've locked on to the one person who can prove he's still alive."

Jayne.

"There has to be another way." A sinking sensation dragged at Heath's conviction that he could make this right somehow. This was way over his head.

"There is no other way. If you fail, finding him again will likely be impossible."

"Why me? Why don't you send a whole team of government agents down here if all you say is true?" How the hell was he supposed to stop a guy like that? How could he protect Jayne if Stephens brought in his team of mercenaries? Heath didn't have that kind of training. He was no secret agent. He was just an ex-cop.

"If Stephens suspects for one moment that I'm involved or that any government agency is aware of his existence, he'll bolt. He has to think this is low level, revenge for his involvement with Leberman. If he believes that he's only going up against a P.I., one who doesn't even have a proven track record, he'll feel free to expose himself. It's the only way."

Heath had known there was more to his selection for this case than his climbing skill and lack of involvement in the agency's past. "But what makes you so certain he won't bring a half-dozen mercenaries with him?"

"He won't take the risk. For nearly twenty years he's kept his daughter out of what he does, anonymity protected him as well as her. A group of mercenaries wreaking havoc in Aspen, Colorado, would draw far too much unwanted attention. Stephens's dirty little world depends upon complete secrecy. He needs it. He plans to keep it by taking care of this business personally and quietly."

"How can you be so damned sure?" Heath wasn't afraid for himself, his concern was for Jayne's welfare. She was totally innocent in all this.

"Trust me, Murphy. I am dead certain and I'm relying on you not to let me down. If you fail, there will be no hope for Jayne. There's no turning back now. The damage is already done."

Heath's gaze settled on the monitor as the call ended.

That was the one thing he and Danes agreed upon without reservation. The damage was already done.

THE SOUND OF THE telephone ringing crashed into Jayne's skull.

She groaned and rolled over.

She didn't dare open her eyes. The throb in her skull warned that it would not be a good thing.

Another ring and her head exploded once more.

She groped blindly over the bedside table, desperate to put an end to the torture. She gripped the receiver and dragged it to her ear with her eyes squeezed shut in hopes of warding off additional pain.

"Hello," she muttered, then licked her lips. Her mouth felt like cotton. If she ever even thought about drinking again she wanted someone to shoot her and put her out of her misery in advance.

"Jayne, you up yet?"

Walt.

She suffered a twinge of disappointment that it wasn't her father calling to wish her a happy birthday.

"Jayne?"

What did Walt want this early in the morning? She popped one eye open and was shocked to discover that it was seven o'clock already. Not so early by her usual standards.

"Yeah, sure…I'm up." She pushed the hair out of her

face and considered sitting up but wasn't sure she could trust herself not to howl with the pain that would surely accompany the move.

"Good. I was afraid after the party last night you might forget that the avalanche advisory had been lifted so today's schedule is good to go."

Today's schedule? Oh, no. Ten o'clock prep class and then a three-and-a-half-mile jaunt on snowshoes at one. It was a beginner-level trek. But that gave her no comfort. She groaned again, certain she would not survive rolling out of the bed much less a dozen enthusiastic tourists.

"That didn't sound too good, Jayne," Walt commented, worry tingeing his tone. "Should I try and find a replacement guide?"

"No, no." She pushed up from the pillows, biting her lip to hold back another groan. This wasn't her usual fare. She led the more difficult ventures into the mountains and backcountry. But she'd promised one of her friends she'd cover this one for her. "I'll be there. Just let me get in the shower and make a pot of coffee."

"All rightie then. See you at ten."

His chipper voice echoed in her ears for a full minute after she'd hung up the phone. How could anyone feel that good after last night?

Jayne scrubbed a hand over her face and dropped it to her lap. Confused, she looked down at herself. To her surprise she still wore the jeans and T-shirt from the party. Why hadn't she changed?

And then she remembered.

Heath had practically carried her to her room. She'd had way too much to drink.

Jayne dropped her head in her hands and wished she could crawl into a hole somewhere.

She sat up suddenly. The idea that he'd put her to bed without undressing her, other than tugging off her boots, didn't bode well. What guy wouldn't have used the opportunity to get a look at her hidden assets?

She groaned again. The answer was simple. The kind of guy who had a job to do, a story to write. One who wasn't really interested in pursuing a relationship. Oh, she almost forgot, and one who wouldn't compromise his principles.

But he'd kissed her. On the cheek, but it was a kiss just the same. She'd felt the pull of desire, the heat simmering between them.

Obviously she'd been the only one feeling it. She'd noticed the way he'd studiously avoided her last night at the party. Whenever she'd looked he'd been across the room or talking to someone else. Her every dance had been with someone else.

Dammit.

She pushed to her feet and trudged to the bathroom. She'd known better than to fall for the guy. At least it was only a superficial prick to her ego. She liked him well enough, but that was all. It wasn't like she'd really gotten attached to him.

She turned on the shower and stared at her reflection in the mirror. That haunted look that always lurked just beneath the surface, the one that had seen too much on the job, was there as always. But there was another emotion, an unfamiliar one, hiding behind the mask of contentment she always wore as well. This one was hope.

For the first time in a very long time she'd hoped for something more. Verged on the point of real trust. Thank God reality had opened her eyes before she'd made that mistake.

Jayne took a deep breath and prayed today's class and winter outing would be enough for Heath. Maybe he'd write his story and move on. Surely he wouldn't wait out a rescue?

One silly little detail that had been nagging at her from the beginning surfaced once more. Why did she never see him taking notes? Or taping interviews with her? For that matter, they hadn't actually had what she would call an official interview. Every reporter she'd ever met took notes. Maybe she'd asked him.

Or maybe she'd just let it go and hope he left soon. The longer he stayed the more likely she was to really get hurt.

And she'd have no one to blame but herself.

TWELVE EXPECTANT gazes watched Jayne's every move as she demonstrated the proper way to prepare for a cross-country snowshoe trek during winter weather.

There were actually only eleven students; the twelfth person present in the Happy Trails orientation room was Heath. He sat at the rear of the classroom, those dark eyes never leaving her.

At least the blush on her cheeks at the idea that she'd practically passed out on him last night gave her some color. Then there was that kiss. How could she be in the same room with him without thinking about that simple kiss on the cheek or the way he'd pinned her against the counter that first night in Rafe's kitchen. Those foolish thoughts inspired a warmth inside her over which she had no control, thus the blush.

Admittedly, she could use all the help she could get this morning since she looked and felt like death warmed over. She had elected not to bother with a morning run since she would need every ounce of energy she could summon for this outing.

Each class participant had received a list of appropriate clothing for the trip as well as the necessary supplies for unforeseen occurrences. All appeared to be prepared. The forecast called for a sunny day with temperatures hovering in the midtwenties. The snow in the area had been groomed ensuring undemanding mobility. This was a level one trip; it didn't get any easier.

"Careful packing is essential," she told the attentive class of mostly older men and women. One couple looked to be in their forties, but most appeared more in the fifty to sixty range.

She covered the proper way to organize a backpack in a few simple steps. As she glanced around the classroom to see if everyone was listening her gaze unexpectedly tangled with Heath's. Something about the way he looked at her made the bottom drop out of her stomach and she totally lost her train of thought.

"Where's the nearest bathroom?"

Jayne blinked. "Excuse me?"

"The bathroom?" the woman repeated.

"Down the hall and to the left," Jayne explained, dredging up a patient smile.

"Not the bathroom here," the lady smirked, "the one on the trail."

The whole group burst into laughter. Jayne couldn't help but laugh as well. The sole person in the room not laughing out loud was Heath, but the amusement in that relentless gaze told her he'd gotten a kick out of the old lady as well. But there was an underlying seriousness in his expression that made Jayne uneasy. Today's schedule afforded little time to consider his odd behavior. Maybe tonight they would have time to talk.

He'd said he had more questions for her…but that had been a ruse to get her to the surprise party. Still, how much of a story could he write when he knew so little about her?

HEATH WATCHED JAYNE chat over lunch with the group of novice snowshoers. He'd selected a table at the rear of the nostalgic restaurant so that he could keep an eye on her as well as the main entrance and the kitchen door.

He wondered about her work at Happy Trails. The variety of trip offerings ranged from easy hikes, like today's, to difficult cross-country routes, backpacking and various degrees of climbing. He couldn't help thinking how boring an itinerary such as this one must be. Such a monumental waste of her extensive talent.

But she didn't appear bored at all. In fact, she seemed to enjoy the group's flamboyance and humor, all of which was so unlike her usual demeanor. Quiet, reserved. A loner to a large degree. Yet there was an energy about her that drew him. What made a vibrant young woman content with the status quo? Why not grab all the gusto while she was young? She certainly was fearless enough. It didn't add up.

There's no one but me.

Self-protection. Survival.

The impact of that realization hit him head-on. She was protecting her father and herself. If she never got close to anyone she didn't have to lie. Not outright anyway. It was the easiest way. No risk. No threat to the last person on this planet who shared her DNA.

Did she even realize that's what she was doing? Pushing the world away for those rare moments with her phantom father? The idea made him sick to his stomach. What had the bastard told her? Had he brainwashed her into thinking the enemy could be anyone, anywhere, anytime?

But she had gotten involved at least once before. Rafe had said something about some guy. A stranger to town like Heath. The memory of that kiss…of tucking her into bed after the party. As tough as she wanted to play, she was still vulnerable. Had some other guy taken advantage of that vulnerability? Heath had an uneasy feeling it wasn't as simple as that.

Forgetting his lunch, he pushed up from the table and sought a more private place to make a call.

The corridor outside the main dining room offered the only privacy from the lunch crowd and an unobstructed view of Jayne's table.

"Altitude Bar and Grill," blasted across the line along with deafening music.

"Rafe, this is Heath Murphy."

"I can't talk now," Rafe fairly shouted into the phone over the loud music and chatter in the background.

"Wait!" Heath urged. "I need you to answer one question."

"All right. All right. Let me go to the kitchen."

Heath waited, his impatience pounding in his temples, while Rafe made his way to the quieter setting of the kitchen.

"Shoot," Rafe snapped. "And make it fast. I got customers waiting."

"You remember telling me about some stranger who hurt Jayne a couple of years ago…maybe last year." Damn. He couldn't remember.

Dead air filled the void that went on for three beats.

"Why do you ask, Murphy?" Rafe's suspicious tone was to be expected. He loved Jayne, wanted to protect her.

"You have to trust me, Rafe, I need to know." Heath held his breath, hoping like hell the old man would cooperate.

"His name was Richie or Richard Rydner. I don't know. I've tried to forget the bastard."

"Thanks, Rafe."

Heath ended the call, not waiting for whatever warn-

ing the guy would surely have issued. His next call was
to Cole Danes.

"Danes."

"I need you to check something out," Heath said
quickly, not wanting to be distracted any longer than
necessary.

"I'm ready."

"Richie or Richard Rydner." Heath could hear the
scratch of a pen on the other end. "He and Jayne had a
thing for a little while a year or so ago."

"This would impact the case in what way?"

"Just a hunch I've got," Heath admitted. "This guy
suddenly disappeared when things turned serious."

Danes hummed a note of disinterest. "Nothing original about that but I'll check it out."

"Could you do it now?"

"It could take some time."

Heath shifted his weight impatiently. "With your
connections you should be able to reach out and touch
someone and get instant feedback."

"Stand by."

Heath leaned against the wall next to the door, his full
attention on the woman under his watch. Hell, he would
have loved watching her even if it wasn't his job. Her hair
was pulled back in that long braid again. She looked
painfully young and completely innocent. His biggest
regret was that he wouldn't be able to protect that innocence.

She smiled at the woman speaking to her and then held
up one hand as if to halt the conversation. The reason be-

came clear as she reached for her cell phone. A look of surprise brightened her face and she grasped the phone with both hands as if the call was both unexpected and thrilling.

Her father.

Heath's mouth formed a grim line. He knew it was him. Damn him.

A little late to be calling and wishing her a happy birthday. A decent father would have called her first thing this morning. Heath watched the happiness dance across her face just as it had the night before last. Late or not, she'd needed it…hoped for it.

"Richard Rydner," Danes said, jerking his attention back to the phone. "Twenty-six, software engineer from Phoenix. He was found dead in his own apartment. Murdered. The police ruled it as a robbery/homicide. The case stands unsolved." The date Danes provided coincided with the time frame of Rydner's involvement with Jayne.

"Bingo," Heath muttered.

"Would you like to share where you think this is going?"

"The bastard killed Rydner to protect himself."

"What?" Danes asked, skepticism in his voice.

"See if you can find any other men in her life who died an untimely death." He was on to something here, Heath was certain.

"She told me she was all alone," he went on. "What better way to ensure she never shared the truth with another human being? Anyone who got too close went away. Giving her all the more reason not to trust men," Heath concluded, more certain than ever of his assessment.

Danes assured that he would do a thorough search of her background as far back as age twelve, but Heath was only half listening.

Someone talking in the room across the hall had distracted him. One of the private dining rooms, he assumed. He forced his attention back to watching Jayne and paying attention to the conversation with Danes.

His instincts wouldn't relent. The voice…*won't be long now. Love you.* The words were barely audible.

I love you.

This time he didn't hear the words, he saw them as Jayne uttered them to her caller.

He was here.

"I'll get back to you." Heath slammed his phone shut and dropped it back into his pocket while simultaneously whirling toward the door across the hall. By the time he burst through he had his weapon in his hand.

One large window on the far side of the room stood open, its sheer curtains flapping in the frigid air.

Heath swore hotly. He'd missed him. He knew it had been him. The hair on the back of his neck suddenly stood on end.

"Give me the weapon." The cold, hard tone was accompanied by the nudge of a steel barrel to the back of Heath's skull.

He bit back another curse. "No way," he ground out.

"Then die."

The cocking of the weapon echoed in the room.

"Go ahead, kill me," Heath taunted, in an effort to buy himself some time. "You're a dead man already, you just don't know it yet."

The barrel jammed harder into his scalp. "You think so? Tell me who the Colby Agency hired to find me and maybe I'll give you a fifty-fifty chance at survival. A gut shot instead of a bullet to the brain."

Heath laughed and told him what he could do with himself, which would be physically impossible in the literal sense.

"What's his name?" Stephens roared. "I want to know who managed what even Lucas Camp could not."

It was now or never. Heath knew he had to make a move. He was dead for sure if he didn't.

A scream and a loud crash near the door provided an abrupt but blessed distraction. Heath whipped around, leveled his weapon. Stephens had anticipated just such a move. He'd already grabbed the waitress who'd entered the room and shielded himself with her.

"Back off," he growled at Heath.

Heath ignored the order and moved in unison with him and his hostage as he closed in on the window.

"Let her go." Heath kept a bead on the bastard but the woman was in the way.

Stephens laughed. "Still too much of a cop to risk the hostage, I see."

Heath resisted the urge to lunge at him. His trigger finger itched to pull back.

Running footsteps pounded in the corridor.

Stephens shoved the waitress at Heath and dived out the window.

Heath stumbled back, catching the woman, but losing his aim on Stephens.

He steadied the lady then rushed to the window but it was too late.

Stephens was gone.

Chapter Nine

Convincing the restaurant manager that he was fine took Heath longer than he would have preferred. Thankfully the waitress had only seen the other man's gun. She hadn't noticed Heath's since her eyes had been squeezed shut in fear as Stephens used her for a human shield.

The manager had assumed the incident was an attempted mugging and insisted on calling the police. Heath barely talked him out of it, doing a little insisting of his own. He'd come to Aspen for a good time, not to deal with a mugging and the police. The mugging attempt had failed, no real harm done. In the end, Heath had won out.

The customer was always right. Wasn't that the motto in the restaurant industry?

Apparently the noise level had been high enough in the dining room that Jayne and her group had been spared the excitement.

As the group gathered their coats and readied to depart for the trailhead, Heath's cell vibrated in his pocket.

He'd set it on vibrate before going into Jayne's class this morning.

"Murphy."

"What the hell happened?"

Heath swore. He should have called Danes back immediately but the manager had taken up valuable time and then there was Jayne and her group. He swore again. This was not a one-man operation. A guy as experienced in this business as Danes should have considered that little detail.

"Our man had a question for me," Heath said flatly, then offered a smile for Jayne as she herded the geriatric group toward the exit.

"What was the question?"

Heath shook his head, still surprised by the audacity of his target. "I can't believe this guy," he muttered, turning away from the folks loading on the tour bus. "He set me up to walk in on him. He wanted me to know he was there. I'd probably be dead now if that waitress hadn't screamed and dropped a tray of glassware."

"The question," Danes repeated. "What was his question?"

Heath stilled. Danes had known this would be coming. He knew this guy's M.O. "He…" Heath swallowed, a new kind of uneasiness making his gut tighten. "He wanted to know your name. Wanted to know who had done what no one else appeared able to do."

Nothing.

Not a single word.

Silence.

"Oh, hell," Heath accused from between clenched teeth. "You *know* this maniac." He moved a few more feet away from the bus, scarcely able to keep his voice down. If Danes was playing games with him, Heath would—

"I don't *know* him," Danes allowed, taking some of the force out of the storm brewing inside Heath. "I know his kind," he added.

"Whatever. I have to go." Heath was sick of both Danes and Stephens. Both had clearly spent too much time in the spook business playing kill or be killed games.

"There's been a change in plans," Danes said, disregarding Heath's comment.

"What kind of change?" Heath couldn't hold up the group any longer. He climbed aboard the bus and claimed a seat at the very back.

"You must know, Mr. Murphy, that the final confrontation is near."

"No kidding," Heath muttered. Jayne glanced back at him and he pushed a smile into place for her benefit.

"I had hoped we could perhaps detain him, question him regarding a number of exploits in his past. I'm sure he knows things this government would very much like to learn."

"I'll do what I can." Heath couldn't make any promises. Stephens was not the kind of prey a mere cop usually went after, especially not alone. And Jayne's safety was Heath's number one priority.

"Don't trouble yourself. I want you to eliminate him.

He represents far too great a threat to risk allowing him to escape."

Shock radiated all the way to the soles of Heath's feet. "Are you saying what I think you're saying?" he asked carefully. No way could he have understood right.

"Your orders are clear, Mr. Murphy. If you get Howard Stephens back in your sights, shoot to kill."

"I can't do that." No way in hell could he simply shoot a man without provocation. "Not unless he forces my hand."

"Take my word for it, Mr. Murphy, he will provide all the provocation you require. Make no mistake. Only one of you will survive the confrontation. The only decision you have to make is whether it will be you or him."

The conversation ended on that note.

Heath closed his phone and dropped it back into his pocket. Funny thing was, he didn't recall any of this being in the vague briefing he'd received prior to taking this assignment.

"Is everything all right?"

Heath looked up just as Jayne took the seat next to him. He smiled, unable to help himself. With her this close he didn't have to fake it. "Everything's fine."

She looked away for a moment. "I thought maybe that was your girlfriend or your wife."

Heath shook his head. "No girlfriend, no wife."

"Good." She started to stand but hesitated and leaned toward him instead. "I would have hated to punch you in front of all these people for kissing me last night if you were already taken."

He watched her go back to the front seat, pausing to chat with one person after another in her group. Damn her father and damn Cole Danes. They'd put him in this position. What the hell was he supposed to do? Shoot her own father right in front of her?

There would be no happy ending to this story.

Only shattered lives.

JAYNE SURVEYED THE group, ensuring everyone was properly suited up for the trek. Just over three miles with a gentle incline of about six hundred feet would be no problem for anyone in this group. As long as no one had fibbed about his or her general health and physical activity level. That was her only real concern in her line of work, especially when dealing with a slightly older crowd. No one wanted to admit they were old.

The driver would come back in four hours to pick them up, unless she called in and specified otherwise.

She made her way to where Heath waited, watching the bus leave the trailhead behind. "No need to worry, Murphy," she teased. "The bus will be back and this one's real easy, a baby slope."

When his gaze connected with hers she saw worry there. Maybe he just wasn't going to be able to deal with this environment at all. She suddenly wished she knew how to make the old hurt he carried around go away.

But she didn't. They barely knew each other, were still strangers really.

No, she amended, not strangers. *Friends.*

He pasted on a smile that didn't reach his eyes. "I'm okay. Don't worry, I won't freak out on you or anything." He reached down and secured his snowshoes, taking a good deal more time than necessary.

She braced her hands on her hips and watched his confident if prolonged movements. "I hope not. You'd be really embarrassed if any of this group had to carry you back to the trailhead."

Straightening to his full height, he laughed and this time the smile was genuine. "You have my word that I'm good to go," he promised on a more serious note.

"Let's get this show on the road then."

He nodded and gestured for her to go first.

"Okay, folks," she called out. "Let's go tramp some snow."

Since all of the participants had been in Aspen for more than twenty-four hours, altitude problems wouldn't be an issue.

Jayne described the terrain as she took the lead, explaining that this trail offered a pleasant and scenic hike, even in the snow.

The trail hugged the wide, swiftly running creek that cut across the ridge. The edges of the water were frozen, the blanket of snow pushing onto those icy ledges like a winter coat. If they were lucky they would see some of the local wildlife, maybe an elk or deer. Preferably no black bears or mountain lions. Though she carried a defibrillator she didn't want to have to use it.

For the next two hours Jayne did what she did best, talked about the beautiful landscape and pointed out the little things most first-time visitors missed. Like the way the sun peeked through the trees and dropped behind the summits of distant mountain ranges.

Today's generous sun had boosted the temperature to a pleasant thirty degrees Fahrenheit. To compensate for the unexpected warm spell, Jayne loosened her parka. She tried not to get caught up in thoughts of Heath. Each time she looked in his direction he was preoccupied with the terrain. She couldn't help wondering if he'd made a game of it, like counting trees or looking for faces in the clouds, anything to keep his mind off whatever ghosts haunted him.

Tonight they had to talk. She wanted to know why he took no notes for his story. Why he hadn't spent more time asking her about her work. He didn't strike her as the type to procrastinate where his work was concerned.

No girlfriend, no wife.

Excitement bubbled inside her at the prospect that he was, indeed, a free man. She reminded that foolish part of herself that he would be leaving and that falling any further for him would be a huge mistake.

Twice she'd fallen hard and lived to regret it.

She should be smarter than this, at least be more romance savvy.

But, in reality, was there anything practical or strategic about love? It just happened—came out of nowhere the same as Heath had.

Maybe the third time would be the charm. Wasn't that how that old saying went?

No, no, no. She gave herself a mental shake. She would not use the word love in the same thought as Heath Murphy. Not safe. Not safe at all.

Besides, how could she possibly ever trust him or any other man with her heart…with the truth about her father? His enemies would go to any extent to eliminate him. He'd told her that dozens of times.

Whatever she shared with Heath or any other man would always be overshadowed by that lie. The same way her mother's life had been. She had died an unhappy, lonely woman.

Apparently, Jayne was doomed to that same fate.

But her father was all she had. How could she risk causing him harm?

She couldn't. It was too much to sacrifice.

Jayne paused and pointed out a deer in the tree line ahead. While cameras were whipped out and amazed whispers rumbled, her thoughts returned to her nonexistent love life. Why did she worry about any of this? If she was to be alone forever as her mother had been, why not take her happiness wherever she could.

Like now.

With Heath.

Her gaze drifted back to him.

He was looking directly at her. A jolt of need roared through her. She hoped he could read in her eyes just how much she wanted him. She was tired of denying herself. He would leave anyway. What were one or two nights of stolen pleasure? The only person who would be hurt was her and maybe it would be worth it. She remembered the way his bare chest had looked, the strength his body radiated and she knew damn well it would be worth it.

No one could accuse her of being promiscuous, but she couldn't be expected to live out her life with no sexual interests. She was a woman, needed to feel like one from time to time. Most of her male friends treated her like one of the guys and that was fine, great in fact, but she didn't want Heath to treat her like a guy. She wanted him to bring out the woman in her.

What was wrong with that?

Nothing, she decided, as she visually measured him once more. Not a darn thing. She could keep her sex life and her personal life separate…just for as long as Heath was in town. That wasn't too much to ask.

HEATH COULDN'T SAY for sure whether it was the fact that the snowshoeing venture was scarcely more than an uphill walk in the snow or that he was fiercely focused on keeping a watch out for Stephens, but he didn't feel the first prick of panic related to the past.

The only urgency he felt was for Jayne's safety.

It felt strange that he would experience such a strong compulsion to protect her from her own father. He needed to stop Stephens, no question. Clearly the man represented a threat to more than just the Colby Agency. But how did he represent a threat to Jayne, other than via the fallout from his chosen occupation?

He'd gone to extremes to protect his daughter, ultimately, of course, protecting himself. But he could have disappeared from her life all those years ago and never returned. That he did at all, taking even that minimal risk, told Heath that he loved his daughter in whatever way a monster like him was capable.

This same man who loved his daughter had been fully prepared to kill Heath today. He'd wanted the answer to his question and then he would have carried out his threat. Heath had no doubt there.

The one thing he didn't understand when he rationalized all else was why the man cared who'd discovered his existence. What difference did it make? A matter of pride? Heath couldn't get past the idea that there was a connection between Stephens and Danes. Why the hell else would Danes order Heath to eliminate the target? Sure, he deserved nothing better, but it wasn't Heath's decision to make.

And so what if he did stop Stephens. There was a whole posse of his followers out there somewhere. Who was to say those guys wouldn't come after Heath and the agency?

He pushed the puzzling questions aside. This was all personal—from Victoria's son to Cole Danes. None of it was coincidence. Heath might not be a trained secret agent but his instincts were honed by eight years of being a cop.

He'd walked into a setup. Gotten trapped in a war that went way back and in which he didn't know the players or the stakes…except for one.

Jayne.

"Ms. McFarland! Stay away from the water's edge!"

The words were no sooner out of Jayne's mouth than she lunged for the woman who'd moved too close to the creek's edge.

His feet were taking him in that direction before his brain assimilated the magnitude of the situation.

The creek wouldn't be deep.

But the water would be killing cold.

With that thought the splash of bodies hitting the water echoed in his ears.

"Get back!" he yelled at two of the men who rushed to the creek's slippery bank.

The men pulled back, discouraging the others from making the same mistake.

Heath hit the water running.

Jayne was up, tugging with all her strength to get the older woman out of the water.

"Help me," Jayne pleaded. Her hair was soaked. He knew without asking that water would have seeped in around her collar and anywhere else where synthetic fabric ended in skin.

Ms. McFarland gasped for air and wailed, "Oh, God. Oh, God."

Heath hefted her out of the water and managed to get back onto solid, snow-covered ground before the woman's weight pulled him to his knees.

"Ms. McFarland—" Jayne knelt next to her "—tell me where the water got in."

The woman looked dazed. "Just my hair, I believe." She pawed her head with one gloved hand. "My hat came off."

Jayne nodded. "Yes, ma'am. We both lost our headgear."

Water trailed down Jayne's face as she spoke but she ignored it. She dug into her backpack and pulled out a solar blanket. Heath helped her wrap it around the trembling woman.

"This will help keep you warm," Jayne explained. "Your hair is wet so you're going to get colder than I'd like, but the blanket will help." She surveyed the woman closely, likely looking for signs of shock. "Are you sure you don't feel wet beneath your outerwear anywhere else?"

Ms. McFarland shook her head. "No, I'm fine. I think," she added shakily.

"Let's get you on your feet."

The rest of the group, who had, thankfully, remained silent despite having moved in close so as not to miss anything, stepped back to make room.

"I'm okay," the woman assured. "Thank God." She looked at Jayne then. "I'm so sorry. I didn't mean to get so close." She shook her head. "These old eyes aren't what they used to be."

Since a Mr. McFarland didn't come forward, Heath had to assume this lady was the one single on the trip. "How about I walk with you from here," he offered.

"That would be very kind of you."

Jayne mouthed a thank-you.

Heath glanced back at the creek and the headgear that had floated off somewhere downstream. He pulled off his own and offered it to Jayne. "I'm not wet," he reminded when she would have protested. "I'll be fine."

She nodded, too smart to argue.

Upon Jayne's radioed request the bus would be waiting for them at the trailhead a few minutes early. The trip back, she warned the group, would be covered at a bit of a faster pace to ensure Ms. McFarland's comfort.

Heath knew there was far more at stake than comfort. Both these ladies were going to be cold as hell before they reached that bus. He wanted to ensure that Jayne was okay, to keep her warm, but she needed him to do exactly what he was doing.

JAYNE IGNORED THE cold that had penetrated her skin, absorbed into her muscles, chilling her all the way to the bone. She couldn't let it show.

They reached the bus in record time. Ms. McFarland appeared to be doing fine. Heath's gaze kept shifting to Jayne. She knew he suspected what she couldn't hide from him.

He was no novice like the rest of this group.

He could read the pain on her face as hard as she tried to disguise it.

She'd twisted her ankle in her attempt to save Ms. McFarland from the water. Nothing was broken, she felt confident. It wasn't even a particularly bad strain, just a nuisance. Something she could definitely have done without.

When they settled in for the ride back to the hotel, Jayne sat down next to the other survivor of the dip in the creek. "Ms. McFarland, I've got an EMT standing by at the hotel to check you out. Is that okay?" Before the lady could answer, she added, "It would really make me feel a lot better."

The woman, who looked frail compared to a few hours ago, nodded. "That would be good." She grasped Jayne's hand when she would have moved away. "Will he be examining you as well, Miss Stephens?"

"I'm fine," Jayne insisted. "Don't worry about me. This isn't the first time I've taken a tumble."

Jayne moved to the back of the bus to sit next to Heath. She sat there for a moment, not sure if she wanted to open this can of worms. He saw through her too easily.

"Thanks for taking care of her," she said softly.

"You're welcome." He turned his head then and looked directly at her. "How bad's the ankle?"

Dammit. She'd known he could read her too well. "Not too bad. A mild sprain. No real damage."

"Why don't we let your EMT have the final say on that?" he suggested quietly.

She pulled off his headgear and relaxed in the seat. She was still freezing but damned if she had the energy to do anything about it. She'd shivered until her teeth rattled. The heat on the bus was slowly doing its job, but not nearly fast enough to suit her.

"Men." She laughed softly. "You always want the final say."

As Jayne suspected her ankle was fine, just a mild sprain. Though she still felt chilled, her body temperature was back to normal and, thankfully, Ms. McFarland checked out A-okay as well.

Jayne couldn't imagine what made the woman wander so close to the edge of the creek. She'd said she hadn't realized she'd gotten that close and maybe she hadn't. No point in overanalyzing it. No one really got hurt and the whole group, including Ms. McFarland, had been abuzz about their adventure the entire trip back to town. There was no telling how many times and different ways this story would be told.

"There is a little swelling," Paul Rice, the rescue team's EMT, noted on his second look at Jayne's ankle.

"I'm fine," Jayne asserted. She wished Heath hadn't insisted that she do this. She knew what would come next.

"Okay, okay," Paul relented as he let go of her foot.

Jayne glowered at him, then she gave Heath the same treatment. She'd managed to get away from the hotel without Paul's knowing she'd been injured. When he showed up at her door only minutes later with Heath she'd known she'd been ratted out by her new friend.

He stood on the other side of her living room trying to look humble. Impossible. She doubted there was a humble bone in his cover-model-quality body. Despite her annoyance at the moment she desperately wanted to find out.

She looked away from him and took a mental step back. Having a one- or two-night stand with him had sounded great in theory but this was real life. She wasn't so sure it was such a good idea. She had too much emotional baggage to be carefree and casual about intimate relationships. The last thing she needed to do was let her lust override her reason.

"Sorry, Jayne," Paul said, dragging her attention back to his big, burly frame. "I'm going to have to recommend that you go on light duty for a few days as far as search and rescue goes."

"I told you I'm fine," she countered as calmly as her irritation would allow. "A hot soak in the tub and a good night's sleep and I'll be as good as new." She had changed clothes and dried her hair but hadn't made it to the tub yet. She needed that soak. Despite the pleasantly warm temperature in her cozy apartment, she was still cold inside. It would take at least an hour of hot, hot water to cure that.

Paul stood, hauling his medic bag up with him. "Don't give me any grief, Little Boss," he said with a pointed look at her. "I could tell Walt that you need a week or two of R and R."

Her mouth dropped open in dismay. "You wouldn't dare."

"Don't tempt me." He grinned. "Keep up your Happy Trails schedule if you feel up to it, but no rescues for two full weeks." He looked from her to Heath and back. "Relax a little. Didn't you just have a birthday?" he asked her, then turned to Heath once more, "And what about you, don't you have a story to write?"

That reminded her.

"Get out of here, Paul," she groused. "I don't need any orders from you. You tell Walt anything about this and I'll make you wish you hadn't."

The EMT's eyes rounded in mock fear. "I'm shaking in my boots." He hee-hawed at his own humor. She merely rolled her eyes. Heath kept out of it.

"I'd better get going," Paul said, apparently knowing he'd worn out his welcome.

"Thanks," she muttered as she drew her knees up to her chest. Damn, she just couldn't get warm. As soon as Heath gave her some privacy, she intended to do something about that. She had some brandy around here somewhere. Maybe she'd start a little fire inside, as well.

Heath closed the door behind Paul and locked it. She didn't know why he bothered with the lock. He would be leaving next.

"Thanks again," she said when he walked toward the sofa. She hugged her legs tighter when another chill shivered through her, but she was reasonably sure this one had more to do with the man watching her than with her recent icy swim.

"Why don't I draw you a bath," he offered, his voice far too soft, too intense.

This was not a good idea. If she was smart she'd give him an unequivocal no.

She looked him dead in the eye and said exactly what she felt. "I'd love it."

Chapter Ten

Jayne shivered at the sound of the water running in her tub. Was she really going to do this?

"How about a glass of wine?"

The sound of his voice as he moved back into the room sent more goose bumps over her skin. "I…" She took a deep breath. "I have brandy somewhere over there."

"Brandy will be even better."

As he prowled through her cabinets, she tried to reason out the whole issue, but too much of her brain was focused on analyzing the way he moved. He'd stripped off his Gore-Tex and Nomex synthetic wear, but he hadn't bothered to go back to his room and change. The cold-weather pants gloved his strong body in such an enticing manner that she could scarcely bear to look. He'd pushed up the sleeves of his oatmeal-colored long-sleeved undershirt.

His hair was windblown and so damned sexy. She swallowed to ease her parched throat. How could she say no to all that? She closed her eyes and chastised herself. Okay, okay, it wasn't just about the great packaging.

Heath was kind and generous. She liked the way he interacted with her friends, especially Rafe. He'd gone right to Ms. McFarland's rescue. No matter how little she knew about him, he was simply a nice guy.

And she wanted so to be with him.

Maybe it was a foolish mistake.

Her father was probably right. She should steer clear of strangers…should protect herself. But she was so tired of doing the right thing.

She wanted to indulge herself just this once.

To be foolhardy and self-absorbed.

Just for tonight.

"Here ya go."

She looked up to find him watching her with those intense brown eyes. She would never forget the pain she'd seen there that day on the mountain. Like her, he had baggage, too. Maybe that was one of the things that attracted her to him.

Her fingers brushed his as she accepted the cup of brandy. She didn't own any fancy stemware other than the one wineglass and it was in the dishwasher. "Thank you."

He nodded. "I should check on your bath."

She watched him walk out of the room, unable to resist that additional pleasure. She wanted this far too much. It had to be a mistake. Nothing this good had ever turned out right in her life.

A sigh pushed past her lips. Well, that wasn't true.

She had her work and the mountain rescue team. She loved living here, enjoyed her friends tremendously. Those were all wonderful things. But those things didn't keep her warm at night, didn't make her feel like a woman.

She needed intimacy, too. She'd gone far too long without it as it was. She'd been so afraid to go out on that limb again…after Richard.

Her college days and that one other big fiasco didn't count, she told herself. Everybody made mistakes at that age. It was a rule of some sort. How else would a person ever learn anything? Risks were necessary.

This was necessary.

She thought about the other girls, some friends, some not, from her high school and college days. Most of them likely had big-time careers or husbands and kids, maybe both by now. She'd shrugged off a graduate degree in favor of being a trail guide. Had all but given up a sex life to be a part of mountain rescue.

It felt safer on those kinds of cliffs and ledges.

But there was something wrong with that picture on the most basic level.

Don't overanalyze, Jayne. This isn't rocket science. It's sex.

She closed her eyes to the count of three and banished all thoughts of rights and wrongs and what-ifs. Then she promptly downed the brandy, cringing at the burn and waiting for the courage it would instill with its warmth.

"Why don't you get in the tub and I'll get you a refill?"

Jayne gasped and looked up at the half-dozen feet of lust-arousing male towering over her. He was too gorgeous. "Sure," she croaked.

He offered his hand for support. She clasped it, feeling the electricity even before their palms touched. He helped her to her feet when she could certainly have managed the feat on her own. She must be drunk already, she mused. Otherwise having a man help her in this way couldn't possibly be so much fun. She usually preferred taking care of herself, being strong.

Tonight she wanted to be vulnerable…weak. She wanted to be needy. She wanted that need filled.

To her credit she walked out of the room without hobbling once. She couldn't deny more than a little discomfort but she wasn't going to own up to it. It annoyed her immensely that Paul had put her on light duty for a few days. She hated when he did stuff like that. When she'd taken her first tumble, garnering herself all those stitches in her leg, he'd put her on six weeks of light duty. Way more than she'd needed. She might be enjoying Heath's attention, but she hated the idea of any sort of weakness on her part getting in the way of her work. But then, setting her injured ego aside, rescues often involved life-and-death situations. Time was always the enemy. Even a mild sprain could waste precious time.

When she opened the bathroom door the steam wafted out to greet her. She liked that. She'd have to remember to keep the door closed that way. Her clothes came off in nothing flat and landed in a pile on the floor. Her hair went up with a handy claw clip. The steam settled on her flesh like a lover's whisper.

Shivering, she eased carefully into the water, moaned with the incredible ecstasy it sent cascading through her body. Any lingering chill in her bones dissipated as she relaxed into the massive claw-footed tub. That was the best thing about this tiny apartment. She wouldn't trade this place and its tub for one of the fanciest condos in town.

The steam continued to hang in the air like fog, adding the perfect ambience to the faint light glowing from the ancient wall sconces that hung next to the mirror. She'd have to thank Heath for this. She smiled. Really, really thank him. She thought of at least a half-dozen ways to show her gratitude.

He tapped on the door. "Would you like that brandy now?"

Her smile stretched into a wicked grin. "Yes, please."

The door opened and he stepped inside. She drank in the sight of him, but couldn't quite quench that particular thirst by merely looking. He set the cup on the little wrought-iron table next to her tub, the one she used for shampoo and body wash.

"Thank you." She reached for the brandy and sipped it, braced her fledgling courage.

"I'll call you later tonight. Let me know if you need anything else."

Her heart bucked against her sternum. He was going to leave. She couldn't let him go…she had to do something or say something.

"Can you stay a while longer?"

God, the request came out all whiny instead of sultry. Couldn't she do anything right?

He hesitated at the door, allowed his gaze to search hers for a time before he spoke. "I'm not sure you really mean that the way it feels like you do."

Dammit. He obviously knew a pathetic job at seduction when he had one thrown at him.

She moistened her lips and summoned her bravado. "What does it feel like I mean?" She downed the rest of the liquid courage, suppressing the need to cough.

He sighed. She held her breath.

"You're beautiful, Jayne, and I'd like nothing better than to climb into that tub with you, but it would be a mistake. I, for one, have already made enough of those for one lifetime."

If she let him go after a confession like that she really was crazy.

She set the cup aside and pushed up from the steaming water. For a second she thought he might bolt, but when she stepped out of the tub he just stood there, staring at her as if…as if he felt torn in some way she couldn't fully understand. *No girlfriend, no wife.* No need to be torn in her opinion.

She walked right up to him and took his face in her damp hands. Before she dragged his mouth down to hers she took a long, slow look…first into those smoldering eyes, then at the planes and angles of that face she'd come to see in her dreams…and then those full lips. Her mouth watered the same way it did when she anticipated the first bite of a delectable hot-fudge sundae.

Her pulse pounded, her heart raced, but she'd never done anything this bold before and she wanted to experience every single moment and detail of it. She tiptoed, moving closer, parting her lips slightly. He held absolutely still, as if he'd read her mind and knew exactly what she intended.

The ache of need was more than she could bear…she had to touch him. She pressed her lips to his, keeping the pressure light, enjoying the sensation of his mouth against her. Warm…firm and smooth. His lips felt good. Heat seared through her, took her breath. She had to have more. She drew his bottom lip between hers, sucked it like candy, tasted the man and the lingering flavor of coffee. She moaned with the flood of sensations that washed over her.

Her hands began to move, to feel, to seek new discoveries. She loved the varying textures of man and material. Her breath came in rapid bursts…his did the same but he held completely still, waiting.

She wanted to feel his naked flesh. As she drew more deeply on his lips, sucking, enveloping, then licking, she tore at his soft undershirt. When her palms found his hot skin the urgency inside her increased to a fever pitch. Her arms went up around his neck and she closed her mouth fully over his, out of patience…needing more.

She'd wanted to make this moment last, to feel it evolve to the next level, but she couldn't slow down the pace. She wanted to experience more of him. She lav-

ished him with fervent kisses—his face, his mouth—
allowed her lips to drag over those planes and angles
she'd admired for days now.

Just when she was certain he wasn't going to respond
at all, his arms went around her. Those long-fingered
hands glided over her wet skin, tracing, teasing. He took
control of the kiss. Touched his tongue to hers, then suckled gently, drawing it into his mouth. She moaned. Buried
her fingers into his thick hair. He learned her mouth with
his tongue, tasted and sucked until she thought her heart
would hammer right out of her chest. The lure and heat
of that wicked tongue made her hungry for more.

He lifted her bottom, pressed her hips against his. He
was hard. A responding desire coiled tighter inside her.
He wanted her. She wanted him. Why had she waited
this long? She should have kissed him the first moment
she laid eyes on him.

She wanted him naked. Right now.

Pulling away from his mouth took all her willpower.
They peeled off his undershirt together, tossed it aside.
He yanked off one boot. Impatient, she dropped to her
knees and removed the other. And then she reached for
his fly, her gaze fixed firmly on his.

He didn't try to stop her, just watched as she tugged
off the pants and then the long underwear the day's adventure had required. She hesitated at the snug fitting
boxer briefs remaining. Her hands trembled just a little
as she fingered the waistband, unable to take her eyes
off the way they formed to his body, giving her a heady
preview of what waited beneath that soft fabric.

She took her time, leaned closer, heard his sharp intake of breath as she kissed his lean hip. Once she'd started she couldn't stop. Her fingers curled into the waistband of that final barrier and dragged the soft fabric down his long, muscled legs. She touched him and he shuddered, balled his fingers into fists and pressed his head back against the closed door. She liked this feeling of power over him.

With more sexual daring than she'd realized she possessed she licked his entire length. The earthy taste of him, the tormented groan he exhaled fueling her confidence. The feel of his hardened length against her bare shoulder made her shiver with anticipation as she kissed her way over his ridged abdomen. Slowly, painstakingly, she licked and kissed, teased his male nipples, then stretched upward, seeking that hot, carnal mouth.

This was no slow, sweet kiss. This time it was urgent, needy and pushed her over some edge that she hadn't anticipated this quickly. He lifted her into his arms and carried her back to the tub. The water had cooled but did nothing to slow the sizzling passion building between them. Water sloshed onto the tile floor as he pulled her down on top of him beneath the water's enveloping embrace. She could feel that hard ridge of flesh beneath her, throbbing, pulsating with need. He pulled her to him, trailed a finger over her breast. She gasped. Wanted more.

He tilted her lips up to his and his hands moved over her now with renewed urgency, making her body mindlessly arch and undulate in search of the fulfillment only he could give. But she couldn't bear to leave his mouth and those mind-blowing kisses, couldn't stop touching his face long enough to do what needed to be done. His hands curled around her waist and lifted her upward, drawing her greedy mouth from his, at the same time, bringing her breast to his mouth. She braced her hands against the rim of the tub and gasped at the feel of his seeking mouth on her breast.

While he pleasured one breast with those skilled lips, he satisfied the other with his hand, plucking her tender nipple, cradling her roundness. Her thighs squeezed on either side of his hips. She couldn't stop that instinctive back and forth movement of her own hips. Every move pushed her closer and closer to release. The feel of his sex pressing against her, hard and smooth, was driving her mad. She wanted him inside her.

As if anticipating her desperation, his free hand slid between her legs, touched her. She cried out, unable to contain the wanton sound.

He shifted his tip into position but stopped her when she would have sunk onto him. She searched his eyes, a question in her own. He cupped her face in his hands and pulled her to him for one more of those slow, easy kisses. Every emotional barrier she kept locked so securely crumbled helplessly.

As precious as that kiss was, her body ached to be filled by him. To complete this mating. He didn't make her wait any longer. He settled his hands on her hips and ushered her downward.

Climax came in a landslide of sensation…of pure pleasure.

He wrapped his arms around her and rolled her onto her back sending more water cascading over the rim of the tub. He held still until she could breathe again…think again and then he started the whole process over again. He thrust long and deep, taking his time, kissing her like she'd never been kissed before. And then she knew why he'd waited until she recovered. He didn't want her to miss anything…wanted her to feel every inch of him, every thrust, until she flew apart in his arms once more and he came with every bit as much force as she did.

HEATH HAD NEVER shampooed a woman's hair before. He liked it. He liked it a lot.

"That was amazing," she said, sitting upright, her legs still wrapped around his waist. He'd lost count of the number of times they'd added more hot water to the tub. They had taken their sweet time washing each other's body, relishing the simple act of touching.

"If you think that was amazing, wait till I do this." He took her hand in his and kissed each fingertip and then the palm of her hand. She sighed dreamily. He was certain he'd kissed every part of her at least twice and still she responded like it was the first time.

"You know," she said drawing his gaze up to hers, "I'd planned to spend this night questioning you."

He leaned back in the tub, loving the hell out of the view. She had a gorgeous body. But that was no surprise. The size and tilt of her breasts were every man's fantasy. He couldn't help reaching out to touch one.

"I'm serious." She batted his hand away.

"Okay. I'll behave." He clasped his hands across his chest and gave her his undivided attention...well most of it anyway. There wasn't a damned thing he could do about the reaction of his sex to her round bottom.

"Why don't you take notes?"

He frowned in confusion. "What notes?"

She folded her arms over her chest, hiding those luscious breasts from his view. "Notes. You are writing a story, right?"

He gave himself a mental kick. "Oh, yes." He shook his head. "I don't need notes." He grappled for some explanation. "I'd rather observe and then tell the story in my own words."

That appeared to satisfy her on that score. "But what about questions? Don't you have more questions for me? Additional background information for your story?"

Now she was worried about whether he was legit. She was running scared. He had to do something about that. A deliberate smile kicked up the corners of his mouth. "I've been asking questions. Just check with your friends, like Rafe."

Her serious expression rearranged into surprise. "Oh." Then she fired off another question. "What did you mean last night when you said forgive me?"

He carefully schooled any reaction to her reminder of his one slip in composure. Forgiveness was something he did not expect...not when she learned the truth.

Dodging her question, he threaded the fingers of one hand into her hair and pulled her close. "Don't do this, Jayne. Just let me make love to you."

She hesitated, then surrendered without a fight. He made it worth her while. He kissed her until they both had to come up for air. With that done, he lifted her out of the tub careful of the numerous towels they'd scattered about to soak up the water.

He settled her on her feet and took his time smoothing a towel over her skin, kissing her shoulder, her elbow…every part of her the terry cloth touched. When her breathing grew as choppy as his own, he swung her off her feet and carried her to the bed. He lowered her to the sheets, his eyes never leaving hers. He wanted her to see how much this meant to him. How much *she* meant to him.

He kissed his way down her satiny skin, pausing to pay special attention to her breasts, something he'd just learned she loved. He traced a scar on her leg with his tongue and made a mental note to ask about that later, then licked and suckled until she quivered beneath his touch…until she begged for him to finish it.

And still he tortured her…tortured himself with the most intimate of acts. He spread her legs wide and tasted her. She arched upward, her fingers knotting in the sheets. He didn't want her to forget the way he'd loved her…had to imprint his touch on her memory. He had to have her until he exhausted himself. He wanted her so much…had thought himself incapable of feeling this way again. It was a blessing and a curse.

He couldn't think about that tonight.

Nothing else mattered…not the future or the past. There was only here and now. He couldn't let it go.

"Please." She reached for him and he could not deny her.

He moved up over her with the knowledge that she was right on the verge of going over the edge. Her body writhed with needy impatience under his. She couldn't catch her breath.

He kissed her cheek. Just like the first time he'd kissed her…before her birthday party.

"No more," she pleaded. Her legs wrapped around his and pulled his hips toward hers.

He pushed inside her in slow, agonizing increments. His entire body shook with the effort of restraint. She clawed his back, surged upward and the control he'd held on to for so long snapped. He pounded into her until she screamed his name…until he followed her over that emotional cliff and altered the landscape of his heart forever.

Chapter Eleven

Inside the Colby Agency

Cole Danes turned off the portable remote observation monitor and pushed away from the desk.

He moved to the wall of windows overlooking the city of Chicago. Lights glittered in the darkness for miles all around him like fallen stars. Maybe there was a single sentimental cell left inside him after all, but he doubted it. More likely his mental waxing was a result of boredom.

He'd underestimated Heath Murphy's self-discipline. He'd expected this physical bonding twenty-four hours ago.

Cole crossed his arms over his chest and tapped his chin. There would be no more waiting, however. Stephens would act at once as he'd done in the past.

Murphy was no fool. Even with next to no facts on the case, he'd figured out the target's motivation as well as his M.O. That definitely merited high marks.

Cole smiled. He'd made the right choice.

Stephens would have no recourse but to reach out to

any and all contacts. He would *need* to know who'd breached his carefully constructed security.

Tonight had given Cole the reassurance he'd needed. Murphy would not fail, nor would he require backup. He would eliminate the target without hesitation. Stephens would provide the necessary motivation...it was his one fatal flaw. His emotions where his daughter was concerned were unerringly predictable. And that would be the death of him.

Then justice would be served on all counts.

Cole turned out the lights and walked out of Victoria Colby-Camp's office.

The next move was the target's.

Chapter Twelve

Jayne lay still for long minutes, watching the morning sun creep into her bedroom. Fingers of golden light reached across the bed, highlighting the masculine planes and ridges of Heath's muscular body. A smile played around the corners of her mouth as she considered how warm and secure she felt in bed with this man. The feeling was so unfamiliar, surreal almost…like a fantasy come to life. He made her feel complete. Complete on some level she'd never known existed before now. She'd felt a kind of bond the two other times she'd fallen for a guy, but nothing to compare with this.

She didn't want to think, she just wanted to enjoy this moment. Overanalyzing was a bad habit of hers. Searching for the hidden agenda behind everything good in her life was growing tiresome. *This* was good. *Heath* was good. Being with him made her feel fulfilled, something she'd been lacking for a very long time.

A soft sigh whispered past her lips. She could look at him like this forever. Shadows still obscured his face but she knew every angle and curve by heart. A day's growth of beard gave him a rugged, almost dangerous air. That smile nudged at her lips once more. She liked his strength, even that hint of mystery that shrouded him.

A reporter who asked few questions. By his own admission he preferred diving into a subject and then writing the story in his own words. After last night, she decided that she liked that strategy herself. Diving in was very, very good, she mused.

Memories of the water sloshing over the sides of the tub, and Heath pulling her down on top of him filtered through her mind like a movie in slow motion. The way he'd kissed her. Her smile widened to a grin. The way she'd kissed him. Boldly, wantonly. Now that was a first. She'd liked that power. Had loved the feel of his skin against hers, of his body mated fully with hers. Soft moans, savage groans, urgent pleas combined with the sounds of their bodies coming together in those final frantic moments. And the sweet, earthy fragrance of their lovemaking.

Heat simmered inside her, making her wet and restless with anticipation, making her want to push him onto his back and climb aboard.

And why not do just that?

She'd decided to go for it. To put aside her usual inhibitions and defenses. There was no rule that said this had to be a one-time thing. They could make love at every opportunity for as long as Heath was in town.

An ache pierced her. Because she was certain that

when he was gone she'd never be able to feel like this with anyone else.

No more thinking.

She smoothed her hand over that awesome chest. His lids fluttered open and those dark brown eyes instantly cleared of sleep and focused on her. He smiled, the sexiest damned smile she'd ever laid eyes on.

"Good morning," he murmured, his voice husky with sleep and with the desire that promptly shimmered in his eyes.

She had done that. Her touch had set him off the same as merely looking at him had done her.

He didn't resist as she pushed him onto his back. To the contrary, he relaxed into the pillow, his arms thrown over his head, those corded limbs resting on either side.

"Don't move," she ordered.

He licked his lips, his gaze settling intently on hers. "Not even if you put a gun to my head."

Raising up on all fours, she straddled him, braced one hand next to his face and leaned down to taste those tempting lips as she simultaneously rubbed her moist heat along his smooth, hard length. "I woke up wanting you," she whispered breathlessly, her voice reflecting the wondrous glow she felt inside at the memory.

He kissed her lips lightly, the same way one tasted wine. A single sip, but with a thoroughness and concentration that involved all five senses. "I woke up dreaming of you," he murmured, each word punctuated with another tender meeting of lips. His hands skimmed her body, leaving a path of fiery sensations wherever he touched. "And here you are."

His words only added to the urgency and it would not be denied any longer. Giving him one last kiss, she shifted her weight to her knees and reached down to guide him to just the right spot. He watched her, the fierce need in his eyes emboldening her all the more. She sank slowly, until her body sealed completely against his and they cried out together. Long moments passed before she could move. Her body pulsed with the sensation of being filled so completely by Heath. *Heath Murphy.* She never wanted to forget his name, his face…or the way he made her feel. She felt his fingers tighten on her thighs as he struggled to do as she'd ordered. She was in charge. He wasn't to move.

When her senses had recovered from the overload of pleasure the deliciously deep penetration had wrought, she began to move, undulating her hips in that age-old rhythm that came as naturally as breathing.

She wouldn't be able to hold out long. The drag of her soft, swollen flesh along that generous, hard length quickly took her to the very edge of climax. She fought it with every ounce of determination she possessed, wanted to hold out, to make him writhe beneath her as she had beneath him last night. She wanted him to beg for her to hurry…to plead for mercy. But release came before she could slow its desperate rush. The sounds of her pleasure burst from her throat as spasm after spasm gripped her. She wanted to curl up against him and revel in the cascading sensations that followed. She refused. Kept moving at that slow, steady pace though her heart thundered and her body shuddered with the aftereffects of release.

He groaned deep in his throat. With monumental effort her eyes opened to watch. His fingers gripped her thighs to the point of pain and his body trembled and shuddered as hers had.

Her name came from his lips in a savage gasp.

She knew what he wanted, but she didn't give in. Slow, back and forth, over and over. Her skin slickened with sweat, as did his. She could feel him throbbing inside her, his control almost gone. Like her, he resisted, wanted to make it last for as long as possible.

She panted, unable to drag oxygen into her lungs fast enough. It was all she could do to keep this unhurried pace. She wanted to...oh...she felt herself coming again.

Too soon.

She squeezed her fingers into fists. No. Not yet.

He murmured something inaudible. Tried to urge her into a faster rhythm with his hands but she refused to surrender.

Color flared behind her closed lids. Every muscle in her body contracted, then shuddered as the ultimate moment of pure physical gratification shivered through her, starting at her center and moving outward like the shockwaves of an explosion.

She couldn't move anymore...the intense pleasure was too overwhelming. Heath pulled her down to his chest and rolled her onto her back. He withdrew to the very tip and thrust deep, driving into her with such force that she lost her breath…couldn't think, couldn't speak. He pumped harder and faster until his own release roared through him.

He thrust again and again, slower this time, allowing the final waves to wash over them, melting every muscle.

Their breathing ragged, they collapsed together, a tangle of trembling arms and legs.

She traced a path on his chest, unable to look him in the eye just yet. "That was like climbing to the very top of the highest, most rugged peak you can find for the first time."

He lifted her chin and smiled down at her. "No." He shook his head. "It was better."

Those three words took her breath away all over again. He kissed her before she could recover. Any possibility of resistance, of going on with her life as before, disappeared like an early morning fog beneath the rising sun.

"Do you have plans for the day?"

She nodded, her smile dragging into a worried frown. "Unfortunately I have to take a small group to the Maroon Bells. Rescues might be off-limits but I can pace myself on this one."

The change in his eyes was instantaneous. He knew precisely what that meant. High elevation, level five, difficult climbing. Definitely not for amateurs. Considerably more arduous than the trek they'd made up to the Alpine Hut. Regret squeezed her heart. "You shouldn't go," she said quickly. "It'll be—"

He pressed his finger to her lips. "If you go, I'm going."

She took his hand in hers. "I don't get that about you, Heath. Why did they send you to cover this kind of story? It doesn't make sense."

There was something new in his eyes when he spoke. Something she couldn't quite read, but it filled her with an emotion akin to dread.

"It had to be me."

Jayne sat up and fished for something to put on. A shirt, anything. "You know, I could use some coffee. How about you?" She tried hard to inject lightness into her tone but failed miserably. He was leaving out some pertinent information and she didn't understand that.

"Sounds great."

She tugged on her tattered robe and shimmied into a pair of panties. She tossed him his cold-weather pants, which had been hung across a chair after getting wet on the bathroom floor last night. "Guess that means you get the shower first."

She wiggled her fingers at him in a goodbye and rushed out of the room. The real world was suddenly pressing in around her, reminding her that her time with Heath was short, temporary. And that something wasn't quite right. Lead filled her tummy. She didn't want to feel either of those things…she definitely didn't want him to see her get all emotional.

Ten minutes. That's all she needed to pull herself back together. She'd be fine. She'd gotten over far worse in the past. Her heart launched an immediate objection.

This time—she had an awful feeling—would be the worst by far.

HEATH DRAGGED ON THE cold-weather pants and several realizations slammed into him at once.

He'd made love to Jayne.

He zipped his fly and closed his eyes in despair. He'd lost all sight of objectivity, had shirked any pretense of professionalism.

But the worst of his transgressions was what he had done to her. She trusted him. Finally. And he was, basically, her enemy. Their lovemaking would only add insult to injury when she learned the truth about him and her father.

Not to mention—he swore hotly—that he'd been so caught up in the intensity of their coming together that he'd forgotten about the camera monitoring her room. He gritted his teeth to hold back the words he wanted to hurl at Danes, who was no doubt watching. Instead, he stormed over to the tiny electronic eye, gave his temporary boss a universal hand gesture he'd have no trouble deciphering, then switched the damned thing off.

So much for his new career.

Heath ran a hand through his hair. How the hell had he let things get this far out of control? Had all those years as a cop taught him nothing? You don't get personally involved with a suspect or a witness. Anyone associated with a case was off-limits.

But he'd screwed up. Let his emotions rule him. Maybe he should have given up any sort of investigative work after the accident.

He headed into the bathroom for that shower but stopped shy of the tub.

A quick inventory of his emotions gave him a start. He mulled over his findings as he cleaned up the mess of wet towels from the floor, his movements on autopilot. He piled them near the door and searched the tiny linen closet in hopes of finding at least one last dry towel. Thankfully he found two. He took one, draped it over the rod that circled the big old claw-footed tub then drew the shower curtain around and turned on the water.

It was the strangest thing. He shucked off his pants and tossed them aside.

Moments ago, when he'd thought about the accident, he'd done so without the usual plunge into bad memories. He shook off the idea, not wanting to press his luck.

Damned strange.

He stepped into the tub and pulled the shower curtain closed. His eyes drifted shut as the spray of hot water sluiced over him. Jayne's image filled his mind. Flashbacks from last night as well as this morning tightened his muscles, made him want to call out to her and drag her into this shower with him. Then the fear intruded, twisting his gut in agony. Not that old familiar fear from his past, but a new one, razor sharp in its own right.

The fear of losing her.

CRADLING A STEAMING cup of coffee, Jayne curled up in the chair in front of her computer. She hadn't checked her e-mail in days. Not that she got any that often. She mostly used the Internet for checking the weather advisories and the news around the nation. She didn't spend a lot of time in front of the television. Somehow she got more out of it when she read it. Or maybe the news anchors just annoyed her.

Her telephone rang and she hissed a curse. Setting her hot coffee aside, she reached for the cordless receiver next to the computer with her free hand. She hated having her first cup of coffee interrupted.

She thought of Heath in the shower and considered that he was one interruption she would have happily tolerated. But she'd needed these few moments of space to get her act back together. She was okay now. She could handle this morning-after thing.

Hell, she was twenty-five. Not a kid anymore. If she couldn't do it now, there wasn't much hope. She'd wanted to be with Heath, facing the consequences was part of the deal.

"Hello." She reached for her coffee and stole a sip that scorched her lips and tongue.

"Jayne."

Her heart rocketed into her throat and she nearly dropped the suddenly too heavy cup. She set it aside just to be safe.

"Dad?"

He'd never called her three times in the space of one week. She prayed nothing was wrong.

"We have to talk, Jayne. It's important."

"Is something wrong?" She held the receiver with both hands, her pulse pounding. His voice sounded so…so flat. This had to be bad news.

"Remember I warned you to be careful of strangers."

She nodded stiffly then blurted, "Yes, I remember. What's wrong? Has something happened?" She ignored the concept that attempted to trickle into her awareness. She would not go there…would not think that.

"It's the reporter, Jayne. Heath Murphy."

Her hands started to shake as ice slid through her veins. At first she couldn't respond, but then she blurted, "No, Dad, you're wrong." She felt so cold. This wasn't possible. No way. He'd made a mistake.

"I knew this would be hard for you. He's…gotten close to you. I've sent you an e-mail containing all the evidence necessary to prove that I'm right. Don't believe anything he tells you. I'm coming for you and then I'll explain everything."

The line went dead but Jayne couldn't move.

Her father had to be wrong.

She pressed the Off button and stuck the receiver back onto its base, her actions automatic. Her entire being had gone from cold to numb.

Her father had to be wrong.

But he'd sounded so…certain. So afraid for her.

She reached for the mouse and clicked to open her inbox.

Her hand trembling she opened the message marked "Heath Murphy." An image filled the screen. A picture of Heath. She scrolled down to the next image. A copy of a Salt Lake City newspaper article: *Woman Falls to Death.* The story described in gory detail how climbing enthusiast Heath Murphy, a homicide detective from Gatlinburg, Tennessee, had lost his fiancée in a devastating accident. The two had set out to scale the Moses Tower, an infamously difficult climb, only one had returned alive.

Tears spilled down Jayne's cheeks by the time she reached the end of the article. This was the accident he wouldn't talk about. The woman had been his fiancée. No wonder he didn't climb anymore.

There was more. Just over two years later. Several articles on an internal affairs investigation involving a Gatlinburg, Tennessee, homicide department. Detective Heath Murphy had been cleared of wrongdoing but had resigned, walking away from a stellar eight-year career.

A frown nagged at Jayne's brow. Was that when he'd decided to go into journalism? It didn't seem likely to her. Lots of guys in law enforcement turned to writing, she argued, mentally ticking off several she'd read about over the years. She recalled at least one homicide detective who had turned to writing after a high profile Beverly Hills murder. But this was different. Heath had represented himself as an investigative journalist, not a novelist. Why hadn't he mentioned that he'd been a cop? She could understand him not wanting to talk about the accident, but his career as a detective shouldn't have been off-limits.

Then she reached the final part of the e-mail. A current dossier on Heath Murphy.

Colby Agency investigator.

The Colby Agency was a private investigations firm in Chicago. He wasn't a writer. Had nothing to do with any newspapers or magazines.

Jayne's hand fell away from the mouse.

Heath wasn't here for a story on mountain rescue.

He was here for her…to learn about her father.

But he'd never asked anything about her father. She blinked. Well, he had asked about family, but just that once. If he wanted to know more about her father why didn't he ask questions?

It didn't make sense.

She closed the confusing document and read the subject line of the new e-mail she'd just received.

Physical evidence.

Renewed dread gelled in her stomach.

She clicked on the message.

Look in his jacket. He carries a weapon. The newest message from her father listed five areas in her apartment that she should check for what he called surveillance bugs. The final part of his message proved the most unsettling of all. *I won't be able to contact you again. With these two e-mails my enemy will know I'm on to them.*

Her heart started to beat faster. Fear tangled with the dread expanding inside her. He couldn't be right. He just couldn't be.

But she had to know for sure.

She got up from the chair, her now cold coffee forgotten. She moved to the built-in bookshelves against the far wall. The books she considered keepers were there. Her small thirteen-inch television and a CD player. She tiptoed and felt along the top of the books on the shelf above her head, the one her father had told her to check.

Her heart stumbled painfully when her fingers encountered a tiny object.

She didn't want this to be true.

Oh, please, she didn't want this...

The object was small and black but even she recognized it as a sort of camera. The eye or lens, whatever it was called, was unmistakable.

She threw it against the floor.

Her fury exploding inside her, one by one she found the surveillance bugs and threw them as hard as she could against the hundred-year-old hardwood.

The water in the shower had just stopped. He would be coming out any moment.

But she didn't care. She shook with the pain of his betrayal. She waffled between wanting to scream and cry and throw up. Her stomach twisted and her eyes filled with tears despite all her attempts to keep them at bay.

She found his jacket, sat down on the foot of the bed and held it for a few moments before she reached inside. Touching the weapon wasn't actually necessary. She'd already deduced from the weight of the jacket that there was something heavy in one of the pockets.

Still, she wanted to see.

A sob ripped out of her throat.

To know without doubt that her father's words were true.

Her fingers curled around cold steel. She withdrew the weapon and stared at it. Black. Similar to something she'd seen on television or in a movie. That's all she could determine. She knew nothing of weapons.

It surprised her that her tears abruptly dried upon making this final discovery. There would be more, she knew, when the numbness wore off.

Her father had warned her.

But she hadn't listened.

He'd told her to beware of strangers. He'd known trouble was headed her way. Had even cautioned her that he feared as much.

Still she hadn't listened.

She'd had every warning, every reason to see Heath Murphy coming.

He'd skated right into her life.

Another pang of hurt ached through her, twisted in her chest.

She had to tell Walt that they'd both been fooled. His friend had lied to him. Heath had lied to her. How had she missed all the signs?

Her eyes closed and the hand holding the weapon fell to her lap. Because she'd needed him to be real. She'd needed him. For months—no years—she had denied that need. To keep her father safe, to protect her heart.

Somehow Heath had undermined her defenses. Had known all the right things to say and do.

Because he'd known who she was before he came.

Fury whipped through her and her eyes opened wide.

He'd likely studied her. Had devised the perfect plan to get to her. To make her vulnerable. So he could get to her father.

Her fingers tightened around the butt of the gun.

She would not let him do this. She had to protect her father.

Private investigators worked for clients, didn't they? Heath's client was no doubt her father's enemy.

A cell phone rang.

It wasn't hers.

She stared at the jacket on the bed next to her.

Heath's.

The bathroom door opened just then. Heath, clad in nothing but a towel, took two steps before the gravity of the situation struck him.

He looked from her to the weapon in her hand and back to her. She watched the muscles of his throat work as he swallowed with considerable difficulty.

"Let me explain."

She shook so hard it was all she could do to stand, but she managed. She pointed the gun at him just like she'd seen in the movies. "Tell me the truth. *Now*."

Chapter Thirteen

Aboard the Colby Agency jet

Cole Danes closed the now useless handheld monitor. He glanced out the window and considered whether or not making this journey to Colorado was of any real consequence. The target would be eliminated before dark, he felt confident. All the key elements had been set in motion.

And yet, his own need for absolute certainty required that he take no chances.

Howard Stephens had played right into his hands. His every move had been choreographed from the very beginning by Cole himself.

Cole had spent his adult life doing this kind of work. He never failed. Once he outlined a scenario, things never failed to fall into place. Heath Murphy's resistance to accept the assignment, his very past had been factored into the profile.

Then there was Jayne, the daughter. She too had reacted exactly as Cole had estimated.

He smiled.

The game was over.

Chapter Fourteen

Heath didn't move a muscle.

"Put the gun down, Jayne," he suggested quietly.

"Tell me," she demanded, her voice quavering, "the truth."

Her hand shook and Heath swallowed hard. He couldn't be sure the weapon's safety was still engaged. To his knowledge Jayne had no experience with handguns, but he wasn't absolutely certain. Some of her mountain rescue buddies could have shown her the basics.

He drew in a steadying breath and held out his hands in a let's-stay-calm gesture. "I don't know what's happened since we made love in that bed this morning," he inclined his head in the direction of the tangled sheets "but whatever it is, it's wrong."

"I know who you are." She blinked rapidly. God, she was going to cry. Regret sliced through him. "But I want to hear the truth from you," she added tightly. "Why did you come here?"

The way Heath saw it he had two choices. He could

keep lying to her and take his chances with her marksmanship or he could tell her the truth and…well, basically risk the same. He was screwed either way.

But none of that mattered.

The only thing that mattered was the way she looked at him right now. The way her eyes glittered with tears. He'd hurt her and nothing he said or did would change that. But he had to try. The idea that this was only the tip of the iceberg banded around his chest making a deep breath impossible.

Obviously they were still in the apartment alone since her father had not put in an appearance. Still, the son of a bitch had contacted her somehow.

"I am Heath Murphy," he told her, letting his hands fall to his sides.

Anger tightened her lips into a bitter line.

"I'm an investigator for the Colby Agency, a private investigations firm in Chicago."

"Why are you here?" she repeated, her voice a little stronger now. But her hands still visibly shook.

Damn, he had to talk her into putting down that weapon or someone was going to get hurt. "Look, Jayne, I know you want answers, but I really need you to put the gun down. You know I won't hurt you."

Her eyes widened with a mixture of fear and fury. "That's just it," she shouted, all semblance of calm evaporating. "I don't know anything. Now, tell me the real truth! All of it," she added before taking a deep, halting breath.

To his extreme relief she lowered the weapon's barrel slightly. At least now if it went off it wasn't as likely to be lethal.

That could very well change with his next statement.

"I'm investigating your father, Howard Stephens."

She flinched but didn't actually look startled. "Why?"

He closed his eyes and blew out a heavy breath. Whatever her father's side of this had been, Heath knew with complete certainty that she was not prepared for what he was about to share with her. "Let me get dressed and I'll tell you everything."

She shook her head. "Don't move, just talk."

Now or never. He had to know just how serious she was. He couldn't risk that she was simply buying time until her father showed up. If he was lucky Danes would be watching via the monitors and would take some sort of action if Stephens made an appearance with Heath in a vulnerable position.

He leveled his gaze on hers. She flinched again. The reaction was like a sucker punch to the gut, because this time it was about him…not her father or the investigation. She didn't want him to look at her. That hurt more than he could have estimated. This situation was totally out of control. His objectivity had gone into the toilet. What the hell. He was standing here naked and disarmed. He had nothing else to lose.

"Do what you have to do, Jayne, but I'm getting dressed. We'll talk then."

Heath turned his back on her and walked into the bathroom. He didn't close the door, just pulled on his clothes and boots without looking back. He ran his fingers through his hair, drew in a fortifying breath and deliberately returned to the bedroom where she waited. The look of devastation that had now claimed her face twisted in his chest, made him want to beat the hell out of Cole Danes and put a bullet in her father's head.

Her father had done this to her.

Cole Danes had added salt to the wound.

Leaving Heath with no way to make it right.

She sat on the edge of the bed now, still clutching the weapon like a rock pick on a slippery ledge.

He sat down in a chair next to her dresser. "I'll tell you the truth but you're not going to like it."

She lifted her chin in defiance of his statement and those big green eyes stared expectantly at him but he could see the hurt quivering just beneath the surface. She'd trusted him and he'd let her down.

Damn his job.

Damn him for letting this get personal.

He was as guilty as Danes or her father.

"Your father isn't in the CIA as you believe. He never was."

A flicker of uncertainty moved across her expression, but she quickly banished it.

When she didn't comment, he continued, "He did work for the military about twenty years ago but he faked his own death so he could disappear."

"That's insane," she countered. Her fingers tightened on the butt of the weapon. "My mother told me about the money the government deposited in her bank account each month. If he wasn't in the military or CIA all those years then why did they pay him? How could he call home or visit if he was pretending to be dead. That's just crazy."

She would cling to any thread of hope as long as possible, but time was running out. If her father showed up...Heath couldn't take that risk.

"Death benefits," he explained. "The government thought he died in the line of duty. They still believe he's dead. Why do you think you're not allowed to talk about him? This is why he wants you to tell anyone who asks that he's dead. Because, to the rest of the world, he is. You're the only one who knew...until a few days ago."

"That's to protect him against people like you," she argued, her words accusing. A lone tear streaked down her cheek. She scrubbed it away, her lips trembling with renewed fury. "People who want to hurt him."

"Your father faked his death and went to work for a man named Leberman."

She went abruptly still. "Leberman?" she repeated.

"Do you recognize that name?"

She blinked then glared at him. "I...No."

Heath tensed. Something about the name was familiar to her whether she wanted to admit it or not. "Leberman operated a team of mercenaries, your father was one of them. Still is, only now he's the one in charge. They get paid to assassinate people. People whose only crime is being targeted by some scumbag who wants to profit somehow from their death. The list of crimes is long, Jayne. Including kidnapping and torturing a child."

She shook her head, her whole body shuddering at his words. "I don't believe you," she argued vehemently.

"His name was Jim Colby. He was taken from his family home eighteen years ago." Heath leaned forward and pressed her with his gaze, needing this next part to hit home particularly hard. He had to get through to her. "This seven-year-old child was kept in a house in Oak Park, in the basement. The torture was relentless."

The color of rage drained from her face. "You're making this up." Some of the conviction had gone out of her voice this time.

Heath straightened. "Why would I do that?"

"To get to my father."

He nodded. "That part's true. My goal *is* to get to your father. He has to pay for his crimes and he may have additional information about what happened to the Colby child."

"Is…" She licked her lips. "Is the boy dead?"

Heath shook his head slowly and moved a step in her direction. "No. He's alive. But he's badly scarred, mentally and physically. Your father helped Leberman destroy his life." He stole another step toward her. "There were many, many others who didn't survive. There will be more unless he's stopped."

She lowered the weapon. Dropped her hand to her lap and stared down at it.

He couldn't bare the despair shrouding her. He had to go to her. He crouched in front of her and reached for her hand. She drew it away. "Jayne, I'm sorry you had to find out this way. I know he's your father and that you love him, but you have to believe me."

Her gaze jerked to his. "Why should I believe anything you say?"

"There's no way I would hurt you with these kinds of accusations if they weren't true." He tucked a wisp of hair behind her ear and she recoiled from his touch. He refused to give up. He had to make her believe him. "Last night meant something to me. You have to trust me. I'm trying to help you. I'm afraid of what your father might do when he learns that you know the truth."

She offered the gun to him and stood. "Get out." She pointed to the door. "I don't ever want to see you again." She pivoted away from him before he could stop her and escaped to the bathroom.

"Wait. Jayne, please."

She hesitated at the door and glared back at him, then moved her head firmly from side to side. "Go. The only thing I want to do right now is wash the lies off my skin."

She slammed the door, shutting him out. He heard the lock slide into place.

He tucked the weapon into his waistband at the small of his back and reached for his jacket. He had to call Danes. A small object in his peripheral vision snagged his attention. He crossed the room to take a closer look.

The surveillance camera.

Within seconds he'd discovered that she had destroyed all five devices. Her father had contacted her and told her exactly what to look for and where to look.

He'd been here—inside this apartment—since Heath's arrival.

Why the hell hadn't Danes warned him?

JAYNE HUNKERED IN THE shower, the tears would not stop. Her body shook so hard she could scarcely breathe.

None of this could be true. Her father wouldn't have done those things.

Heath…oh, God. How could he do this to her?

She'd scrubbed her skin until it felt raw.

She drew in a shuddering breath but couldn't manage to get enough air into her lungs.

She pressed her forehead to her knees and inhaled slowly, deeply, once, twice, three times. She couldn't hide in here forever. She had to get dressed and get to work, had to pull herself together.

That was the one thing she could count on. Her work. Her friends here in Aspen—Rafe and Walt and the others—they were all she needed. She didn't need Heath or her father.

Her father was never around anyway. Fury tightened her lips.

Memories of the way her mother had grieved tumbled one over the other into her mind. She'd talked of his desertion. Of how he had loved his work more than her or Jayne.

But Jayne had always pretended that he loved them too much and that that was why he'd stayed away.

She thought of her childhood home in Oak Park. Of the terrifying basement she'd only dared to visit once. Her father had taken her down there and told her never, ever to go down there again. That it wasn't safe.

Leberman.

She didn't know why the name felt familiar to her, but somehow it did. She shut off the cooling water and concentrated hard. Had she heard her father talking to someone named Leberman? Had her father mentioned the name? Or maybe she'd encountered someone at college or in her work with that name. She just couldn't remember.

But one memory stood out in her mind so vivid that it took her breath every time she dared let it creep into her consciousness.

The little boy.

She remembered a boy, maybe the same age as her at the time…six or seven.

Her father had gone away after she'd seen him with the boy. Her life had changed forever. She and her mother had abruptly moved from their home and never looked back. All the way to California.

Why had she never thought of that boy again… until now?

Leberman.

A cold hard fist of panic slammed into her stomach.

Her father had said the boy was Leberman's son. She remembered that now.

Wait.

Her heart fluttered, sending a new rush of emotion to her stinging eyes.

She shook her head.

She wasn't sure about that.

Maybe she was confusing her vague memories. Maybe part of her wanted so desperately for Heath to be the real thing that she was turning her father into a monster.

Wouldn't her mother have told her about any of this? Jayne had been just a child, but her mother would have recognized the lies...wouldn't she?

Or maybe, like Jayne, she hadn't wanted to see.

Jayne jerked the shower curtain back and climbed out of the tub. She didn't want to think about this anymore. Heath was a stranger. One who had lied to her repeatedly. Had used her. How could she possibly believe anything he told her? What kind of fool did he think she was? Her father couldn't be the monster he portrayed him to be. That simply wasn't possible. She squeezed her eyes shut and forced away the nagging voices that suggested otherwise.

She had a life. She had to get back to it.

Maybe she would be better off if she never heard from Heath or her father ever again.

Forcing a calm she didn't feel, she dressed for work and gathered her gear. She hissed a curse when she glanced at the clock. There was no more time to dawdle. Walt would likely be wondering where she was. None of this was about her. She had to remember that, shove it away. To hell with Heath Murphy and to hell with her father. Let them figure out this insanity.

Her arms loaded with her gear she moved to the living room in search of her boots.

Heath sat on the sofa.

A new blast of anger bolted through her. "I thought I told you to leave."

"I can't."

She rolled her eyes and threw her gear, onto the floor. Dammit she'd had enough. "Get out now before I call the sheriff."

Heath stood but made no move toward the door. "Finding your father isn't the only reason I was sent here," he said firmly. "I'm here to protect you from him. I'm not letting you out of my sight."

Her mouth dropped open and she made a sound of disbelief. "What's your game now, Murphy? Do you think you can frighten me and I'll pretend you didn't lie to me? That you didn't have sex with me just to get close to me so you could find my father? You keep talking about the truth, well I know the truth. The truth is you started flirting with me right from the beginning, I was just too stupid to see it." She flung her arms outward. "This whole thing was just a game—a ploy—to help you get what you wanted! Well, I don't want any part of it."

Heath closed his eyes for a moment before he responded. She wanted to hit him. The urge was very nearly irresistible. She hugged her arms around herself and fought off another wave of knee-buckling emotion. Dammit. How could he still make her feel this way? Make her feel drawn to him? After all he'd done.

"I didn't have sex with you to get close to your father," he said softly. "I made love to you because I wanted you more than anything I've ever wanted in my life."

Her pager sounded, the ominous tones jerking her attention down to her waist.

She turned away from Heath and grabbed the phone, automatically punching in the numbers. "What's up?" she asked crisply.

"Jayne." Walt's voice. "We need everyone to come in ASAP. It's a bad one."

"I'm on my way." She depressed the Off button and pitched the phone onto the nearest chair.

"What's going on?"

She leveled her gaze on Heath. "Mountain rescue's been called out. I have to go." She held up her hand when he would have moved toward her. "I told you to go. Don't come near me again."

She jerked on her parka and boots and gathered her gear.

Heath still stood there, watching her, when she'd finished.

"I'm not letting you out of my sight," he warned. "I told you that I came here to protect you and that's what I'm going to do."

"Get out of my way."

He stepped aside but followed when she walked out the door. She ignored him, just kept moving forward. If she'd hesitated for a single second she might…she just might have let herself be stupid enough to believe him.

"Be careful out there, Jayne," Rafe called to her as

she passed through the bar. Rafe's scanner had likely already warned him of whatever incident had occurred.

"I always am," she tossed back without looking his way. If he got a look at her face he would know something was going on and she just didn't have time to deal with that right now.

Lives were at stake.

She had to focus.

THE MOUNTAIN RESCUE headquarters on Main Street was crawling with activity when they arrived. Heath had followed Jayne in his rental since she refused to let him ride with her. Not that he could blame her.

Two county sheriff's deputies and more than a dozen mountain rescue volunteers were already on site. Walt Messina was outlining the search area on a topographic map.

Capitol Peak.

Not good.

Heath had never climbed, other than his little trek with Jayne, in this area, but he'd heard of that peak. It meant several things to him. High elevation, rugged terrain, tough going even in summer months. Those most likely to attempt such a climb would be skilled; if they couldn't get back down there were injuries or worse. The situation would be dire.

"Why can't the chopper just drop us in on this ridge?" Jayne pointed to a place on the map.

Paul Rice spoke up, "*Us* would not include you, Jayne," he said flatly. "You're on light duty."

She wheeled on him. "My ankle doesn't even hurt," she protested.

"That may be," he allowed, "but that doesn't mean it'll hold up under this kind of physical strain."

Heath watched the tension escalate several notches. All other eyes were on the two, as well, waiting to see how this would play out. Heath knew that Jayne was one of the best climbers the team had. To leave her out was a major call.

"You're out, Jayne," Walt seconded.

"Walt, you can't do that!"

"It's done," he said, his tone final. "Now, let's not waste any more time."

Jayne backed off. She wouldn't let her own ego get in the way of saving lives.

"The call came in about an hour ago," one of the deputies said. "One of the climbers, a fellow by the name of Carter, managed to make it out, found his way to Tom Barker's dude ranch and called for help from there. Apparently the cold got the batteries in the cell phones the group carried."

"Any of them wearing transmitters?" Walt asked.

The deputy, Lebron Littles, shook his head. "But the one who walked out gave us the location of his friends. He says a couple fell and the others got trapped trying to rescue them. He stayed back to go for help if necessary."

Heath understood that there was always room for doubt in any story, but Deputy Littles sounded less than sold on this particular one.

"Do we have any other information on this group?" Jayne asked, determined to be a part of the operation. "Anything that would indicate trouble?"

"Four males, two females. All worked together. This was some kind of business retreat," Littles told her. "But…" He inhaled a heavy breath. "This guy seems a little jumpy to me. His story has changed two or three times." He shook his head. "I don't like it."

"All right," Walt said. "To answer Jayne's original question, we can't use the chopper because of the storm brewing around those peaks. We may get as much as fifteen to twenty inches of snowfall in the next two hours." He shot Jayne a look that said he'd expected her to know that. "The weather advisory was issued early this morning."

Jayne felt the bottom drop out of her stomach for the third time this morning. She always, always checked the advisories…but this morning she'd been distracted. She pressed her lips together as anger, as much at herself as at Heath, swelled inside her once more. She'd let him…let this whole situation affect her work.

Lives depended upon her and she'd messed up.

She shot him a scathing look.

To his credit he didn't look away but that only made her angrier.

Walt laid out the plan in his usual thorough manner. The hasty team would leave immediately. Paul Rice, Chad Wade and four others would lead. The support team would follow. The one climber who'd walked out this morning wouldn't be able to assist since he was suffering from moderate hypothermia. He'd been taken straight to the hospital for treatment. The deputy's suspicions about his explanation of how these events had played out would have to wait.

"Jayne, you'll run the operation from here," Walt told her. "Mason and Snyder will stay behind as well in case anything comes up."

"Yes, sir."

She hated like hell to see the team go without her. Especially Walt. He was good. Damn good, but he was fifty-two. This kind of rescue would be hard on him. She should be leading. It had nothing to do with ego and everything to do with worry about the man.

"Walt?" she called, stalling him at the door. "Be careful. I've got a feeling this one isn't going to be easy."

He nodded and then he was gone.

Deputy Littles patted Jayne on the shoulder. "I'm gonna update the sheriff. He wanted me to keep him posted."

She nodded and dragged her attention back to the task at hand. In fifteen minutes she would conduct a communications check. When Walt and the team reached the trailhead, he'd make contact once more before setting off. Adrenaline surged. She hoped like hell the storm would hold off until this was over.

"Mason, get an update on the storm. I want to know if there's any chance it's going to blow over."

"Gotcha, Little Boss."

She smiled. Dammit. She didn't know why. She

didn't have a single thing to smile about. But something about the ordinariness of him calling her that or maybe it was simply the realization that she was needed here made her lips lift into that stupid smile.

"How about some fresh coffee?" Snyder offered.

She sighed. "That'd be great." She hadn't finished even one cup this morning. She could definitely use some caffeine about now.

A phone rang and she turned just in time to see Heath pulling his cell from his pocket. She remembered it ringing earlier. He moved to the other side of the room to answer and she turned away.

Why didn't he just go? Having him here was nothing but a constant reminder of the mistake she'd made. Something deep inside her went very still.

No. His presence meant a great deal more than that. He was here to apprehend her father, if anything he said could be believed. Her father had told her he was coming. What would happen then?

Heath would do his best to bring him down and her father would likely do the same.

Someone would be hurt…or worse.

Jayne closed her eyes and braced against the worktable for support. She'd let Heath inside her, physically and emotionally. They hadn't used protection, which presented numerous problems of its own. Problems she couldn't even bring herself to consider right now. She'd trusted him, fallen for him. And he'd used her.

But was he the bad guy here?

How could she believe that her father, the man she'd

worshiped from afar since she was old enough to look up to him, was such a hideous villain?

Her mother's haunted image kept nudging into her thoughts. Her father had destroyed her mother. She'd always known that, had held that against him in a sort of way, still did. But he was her father. All she had left in the world and she'd forgiven him that grievous error for the most part. He'd had a job to do. She'd told herself that he was some sort of hero out saving the world all those times he'd left her and her mother behind.

How could all that she'd believed in, all that she'd clung to, be a lie? Hurt squeezed her heart, knotted in her stomach.

She opened her eyes and settled her gaze on Heath.

Every man she'd ever trusted had let her down. Lied to her.

Could she possibly, as much as her heart yearned to, trust this man for even a second?

Chapter Fifteen

The snow had started to fall, gently, innocuously. Estimates went as high as two to three feet over the next twenty-four hours. But there would be nothing gentle or innocuous about the winds combined with that snow at the higher elevations. Visibility could drop to nothing.

For Jayne and her mountaineer comrades left behind, the advisory meant that they could be living at this cabin headquarters for the next few days.

Heath had every intention of staying put wherever she was, whether she liked it or not.

These kinds of weather conditions could lead to more hikers and climbers becoming disoriented and lost. Mutual aid calls would be required, summoning rescue support, volunteer and otherwise, from surrounding communities. Heath knew the drill. All too well.

He'd spent the last hour fighting the panic trying to take root. It was as if he had no control over his own body.

He'd been here before. Watched the flurry of activity that could prove futile. Nothing anyone could have done had saved *her*...and it had been entirely his fault.

His palms started to sweat and he sucked in another deep breath. He knew what he had to do at times like this, knew all the steps for fighting this kind of inside attack. But none of it appeared to work at the moment.

He had to find a way to focus.

Howard Stephens could show up at any time. Jayne was in a public place, one over which Heath held no dominion. He was an outsider, here merely as an observer. Under present circumstances he knew with utter certainty that if he got in Jayne's way she would have him taken away by the sheriff's deputy standing by as incident commander liaison. Heath had to tread carefully here.

A damned panic attack was the last thing he needed.

Heath kept his respiration slow and deep and his attention centered on the woman in control of the moment.

Jayne Stephens was a natural born crisis manager. As report after report of worsening conditions squawked over the radio she grew calmer and calmer, fully focused, completely committed. Not the first sign of panic.

He couldn't help admiring her. Despite the worst kind of father, she'd turned into a true champion, a heroine. She had every right to be bitter and cynical and yet she was neither of those things.

Until Heath's arrival, her life had been content. He'd noted that before. He'd taken that from her. No matter how this turned out, she wouldn't be able to escape the cynicism this time. She would be left hurt and bitter. But she was a survivor. That was quite clear. If her devil of a father didn't get her killed, she would carry on. Heath was dead certain about that. She would not let down her friends or her community. Only her feelings would be damaged…her heart. And Heath was neck deep in guilt for having taken part in that travesty.

He pushed the thought away and counted heads again. He had to stay on top of the situation, had to remember what he was here to do. He had his orders. Stephens had to be stopped. And he would be coming. It would have been nice to believe the man cared about his daughter, but Heath doubted that. More likely he would want her out of the way so that no one could reach him via that route again. Oh, she wouldn't like that one little bit. He wondered how her father would react when she told him to forget it. That she wasn't going anywhere.

She had a life here…one Heath's assignment had turned upside down.

He'd tried to reach Danes twice this morning with no luck. He glanced at his watch. He hadn't been able to reach anyone. It was past time someone had come into the office at the Colby Agency. He'd gotten a call back from the answering service but nothing else.

Trying again, he took a step back from the group monitoring the ongoing rescue, pulled out his cell phone and punched the appropriate speed dial number. The call was answered on the first ring.

"Elaine, this is Heath Murphy. I need to speak with Mr. Danes."

"I'm sorry, Mr. Murphy, but Mr. Danes is not in the office as of yet."

Heath definitely hadn't expected that response. "How about Ian or Simon then?" He had to update someone on the situation here since Danes hadn't called him last night or this morning and Heath hadn't been able to reach him. Where the hell was everybody?

"Ah…Mr. Murphy, there isn't anyone else here except me."

Uneasiness trickled through Heath. "What do you mean? What about Mildred?"

"Mildred left a message for me that she had to go out of town on a family emergency. That's all I know."

"Fine." Heath considered what he should do. "Just have Ian or Simon call me if Mr. Danes doesn't come in. I need to talk to one of them." What were the odds that reaching both men would prove impossible? Sounded like Danes's work to him.

"I will, sir."

Heath closed his phone and dropped it back into his pocket. It seemed impossible. Though it was Saturday, Danes had put the entire staff on a seven-day workweek until further notice. Another of his interrogation tactics. Yet, there was no one at the Colby Agency. Not even Mildred. Mildred was always the first to arrive and the last to go…it didn't make sense.

"If the storm hits as hard as expected," Snyder said, his voice somber, tugging Heath's attention back to the here and now "we'll have to call 'em back."

Jayne shrugged. "Maybe. But it's not like we don't know where these people are." She studied the map again. "If Walt and his team can make it in they can provide emergency medical care and dig in for the duration. Walt knows how to sit out a storm." She studied the incoming weather reports once more. "At least that way maybe these folks will have a chance of surviving."

"Have we heard anything from the request for backup from Fort Carson?" Mason, another of Jayne's mountain rescue teammates, wanted to know. "With those all-weather helicopters they could fly these people out no matter what the storm does."

"The base is already supporting a couple of other rescues," Jayne said thoughtfully. She rubbed at her forehead, the first indication of stress Heath had seen. "I'm hoping they'll get to us soon," she added.

"Walt can lay low if need be until then," Mason allowed. "Like you said, Jayne, he knows how to handle this."

"I just hope it doesn't come to that." Jayne chewed her lip. "I think maybe I'll give the base liaison a call and get the latest on their ongoing ops."

All three were restless, wanted to be out there in the field helping instead of stuck in this cabin coordinating. But the job they carried out was essential. Walt and his teams would be helpless out there without proper support on this end. What Jayne did in here was every bit as important as those making the trek up to that peak.

More rescue volunteers wandered in as the time crept past. Unfortunately for Heath they weren't alone. The media had discovered the drama and converged upon the rescue headquarters. Dozens of cars were parked along the sidewalk outside. From what Heath could determine the Denver company that employed the injured and trapped climbers was of more than casual interest to the statewide media circus, especially considering one of the victims was the CEO. Snyder and Mason kept the growing crowd apprised of the situation. Heath's primary concern was not only to keep an eye on Jayne but also to monitor every new face that bobbed into the scene.

Not so easy with reporters swarming like bees in search of the nearest hive.

"Jayne."

Jayne looked up at the sound of her name, time and place slowly coming into focus. She'd been studying the maps and weather radar screen so closely for so long she'd lost track of the goings on around her. She'd been vaguely aware of the arrival of the media. Perfect.

"Yeah, Lebron, what's up?"

Deputy Littles sidled up to her, closer than necessary, sending her on instant alert. "I've got the sheriff on the line."

She noted the cell phone in his hand then. "Is something wrong?" Her first thought was that there'd been a slide somewhere close to Walt that she hadn't heard about yet. She hated when ICS, the incident command system, worked against her like that. Base operations here needed the information first, not the sheriff's office.

The deputy offered her the phone. "I'll let him explain so there's no confusion."

Jayne took the phone. "Sheriff, this is Jayne Stephens. Do you have information that affects my team in the field?" She walked away from the buzz of ongoing speculations and calculations, more to gain some privacy than to hear better.

"Jayne, I have a situation that I'm not comfortable putting through normal channels."

"Okay," she said slowly. Jayne wasn't sure how the sheriff expected her to respond to that comment. In her three years as a part of mountain rescue she'd never encountered a situation not appropriate for normal channels.

"Dispatch received a 9-1-1 call ten minutes ago regarding an injured climber."

A frown worked its way across her forehead. "Why wouldn't you want that call to come through normal channels?" If they had another victim out there they needed to know. "Is this one related to the ongoing rescue?"

A heavy breath hissed over the line. "No." The sheriff swore softly, surprising her. That wasn't like him. "Just as quickly as I clear one heap of trouble another one drops in my lap," he explained. "Our man, Carter, has come clean and finally admitted that he and the CEO had fought. The CEO slipped over the edge and the rest pretty much went down as Carter had reported. He knows this is his fault and he left the group with the intentions of running. By the time he'd made it to Barker's dude ranch guilt had changed his mind and he called in."

Jayne couldn't help wondering why that mattered just now. She had a rescue to oversee and this was nothing more than a waste of her time, but she didn't see any reason to tell the sheriff that. He had to know it. Clearly he was under a lot of stress here, but who wasn't?

"I'll let you know as soon as Walt reports in," she said for lack of anything else to say. "They probably won't make contact for a while yet." If the CEO was dead, Carter would be up on manslaughter charges, she estimated. Between now and then she imagined the guy would be sweating bullets.

"That's not why I called," the sheriff said, surprising her all over again.

Now she was really lost and she definitely didn't have time for this.

"The other call, the one that came in about ten minutes ago."

Damn. She'd forgotten he even mentioned another call. She massaged her temple and forced herself to pay attention to the conversation for a few minutes more, but her mind was on Walt. She should be the one out there, not him. "An injured climber?" she asked.

This could mean sending another group out into the field. Just what she needed.

"The caller said he had fallen and broken his leg. The connection was bad. I've played the tape twice and I scarcely made it out myself."

"What's the location?" Jayne hurried back over to the map as the sheriff called off the information. Not such a bad place to be stuck even in weather like this. The retrieval wouldn't be that difficult, but it would require expertise and a strong knowledge of the area since visibility would be seriously limited.

"I'll get a team right on it," Jayne told him. This was easy compared to what Walt was going through. She didn't understand the sheriff's strange behavior on this one.

"I guess the thing that strikes me as odd," the sheriff said at last, "is that the guy asked for you by name and the call registered as having come from Thurman McGill's cell phone."

Now that got Jayne's attention. Victims didn't usually ask for rescuers by name. Even stranger, Thurman McGill was a local resident they called upon quite often for air support. Thurman owned two helicopters, used them for giving tourists aerial tours. She supposed Thurman could have asked for her but more likely he would have asked for Walt.

"Did he crash?" That didn't seem reasonable to Jayne. Why would he have been out in this weather? Unless the storm came on more quickly than he'd expected.

"That's just it, Jayne. The voice didn't belong to Thurman McGill. I've tried calling the number back, in case it was a mistake. That happens once in a while, a number will show up as one thing when it's really something else. No system is perfect. There was no answer and I didn't get an answer at Thurman's place either. I sent a deputy over there and nobody's home."

"I'll get a team headed up to that location right now, Sheriff. Keep me posted."

"Jayne," he said, waylaying her, "I don't like this. Maybe you'd better send Littles along, too. I'll send another of my men to cover things there."

She glanced at Lebron. He was a pretty good mountaineer. She didn't have a problem with that. "All right. Thanks, Sheriff." She passed the phone back to the deputy.

"Mason, Snyder." Jayne gestured for the two senior team members present to join her.

"Walt just checked in," Snyder informed her. "They've made contact with the fallen climbers. And Fort Carson called, they've got a Chinook headed Walt's way. He had a time getting over the Continental Divide, but he thinks he can rendezvous with Walt's team within the hour."

"Excellent." That was definitely good news. The Chinook was a large enough helicopter to turn this hazardous rescue into a walk in the park. "Did you pass that along to Walt?"

He shook his head. "Just got the call. I'll do that now."

"In a minute." Jayne took a breath. "I'm leaving you two in charge here." She looked from Snyder to Mason. "You've done this before with me and Walt. You know the steps. Deputy Littles and I are going to follow up on a 9-1-1 the sheriff received." She quickly outlined the location on the map and filled in the sketchy details the sheriff had provided.

"You sure you can handle this with only the deputy?" Mason glanced toward the officer in question.

Jayne nodded. "I've worked with Lebron before. It won't be a problem. He and I should be able to secure this guy. If we can't get him out you can send that Chinook for us when Walt's team is taken care of." She grinned. Mason and Snyder were well aware that the route she would need to take was child's play for her and she had the proper emergency medical training to secure the victim.

"Wait a minute," Snyder said, his expression turning wary. "Rice said you were on light duty. As simple as this rescue sounds, it isn't light duty."

"I'm fine." She gave each of them a stern look. "There's no time for this. Take care of things here, Lebron and I will handle this one. If anything else comes up have the sheriff's office call for mutual aid. Two other mountain rescue units are already on alert status. You've got a few more good volunteers here but I want you or Snyder manning this base. No one else." On second thought, she added, "Keep this second rescue under wraps for now. I don't think the sheriff wanted the media to get wind of it just yet."

Snyder and Mason assured her they would handle things here. Jayne had known Thurman McGill since she'd arrived in Aspen. As a widower, he lived alone. She didn't want to consider whether he might have run upon foul play. It wasn't impossible that he would ask for her rather than Walt. She'd coordinated the use of his helicopters before.

"What's going on?"

She and Deputy Littles had started for the equipment room when Heath's voice reminded her that he was still there.

All that had happened that morning came rushing in on her at once. Jayne closed her eyes and blocked the emotional landslide. She didn't want to feel this, couldn't deal with it right now.

She opened her eyes and looked straight into his. "I have a job to do. Just stay out of my way."

Heath stepped close, intimidatingly so. "I told you that I'm not letting you out of my sight."

Deputy Littles laid a hand on Heath's shoulder. "Back off, sir," he ordered sternly.

Heath stared at the man's hand and then at the man. "That's not happening."

When the deputy's other hand moved toward his holstered weapon Jayne knew she had to do something. "It's okay, Lebron. Mr. Murphy might be of assistance to us." Her gaze leveled on Heath's. "We're headed up to do another rescue. If you're up to it, we could use you." A line of fury burned through her despite her best efforts to keep her mind away from personal issues.

"But if you're not, stay out of the way because I'm not letting anyone die today because of you."

Heath didn't have to answer, she saw the hesitation in his eyes a split second before he banished it. "Wherever you go, I go."

"Fine, just don't get in the way."

Jayne had to admit, this was the most unlikely rescue team she'd ever led but there was no time for over-analyzing. She couldn't leave Mason and Snyder shorthanded. The remaining volunteers were needed here. Another call could come in. Walt's team might need additional backup though she doubted it with the Chinook en route.

This injured climber was her problem. She could drag him out alone if necessary. Deputy Littles was more for that other unknown element than for anything else. On that same note, she had to confess that having Heath come along wasn't such a bad idea. No one attempted a rescue alone. Not even a climber as confident and, at times, as cocky as her. It was the first rule of rescue.

Create no new victims.

CLAD FOR THE WORST winter weather and wearing emergency packs loaded with the necessary supplies, Jayne led the procession from the trailhead. Deputy Littles had driven his SUV, updating the sheriff as to their plan en route.

The weather worked its will as they set out, the wind howled and the snow drove hard into their faces. Goggles protected their eyes. Mere humans, who had any common sense, acceded to the weather's demands on days like this. But Jayne knew that plenty of folks would venture out just the same. They had paid for a holiday in winter's paradise, and they intended to have it. So, with little experience in the mountains those cocky few would venture into the twilight zone made accessible by bravado and Gore-Tex. If they were lucky they survived their stupidity. For others, mountain rescue volunteers such as herself would forage out into the deadly weather and drag them back to civilization.

Jayne had insisted on breaking trail, tromping through the fresh layer of snow, each step plunging all the way up to her knees, slowing her forward movement. But she'd be damned if she'd do this any differently just because the man she'd slept with last night wanted to play the big bad protector.

Heath stayed right behind her, forcing the deputy to bring up the rear. Littles didn't like it and Jayne didn't have time to care.

She kept thinking about Thurman McGill and wondering why he'd asked for her and why the hell he'd gone out on a day like today. Maybe he'd heard that Walt and the others were already out on a rescue and had hoped to help, but that didn't make sense either since he would have taken a different route for that purpose. And he, of all people, was well aware of his equipment's limitations. She'd know soon enough.

It took barely more than an hour to reach their destination. Heath stopped her when she would have continued up onto the ridge. "I'll take the lead from here," he said, his tone brooking no argument.

In spite of her determination not to, Jayne had spent the last hour working hard not to think about the things Heath had accused her father of. She'd come up with a dozen different scenarios and excuses that explained every little thing his accusations had caused her to remember. She'd found no solace. As much as she cared for her father, she would have some answers. If he had done these things…she shuddered and pushed the horrible possibility aside. Not now. She couldn't go there.

Another thing she'd done in the past hour was to talk herself out of love with Heath Murphy.

Love.

God, how could she let that word even wiggle its way into this crazy mixture?

She couldn't…wouldn't. Whatever they'd shared was over.

"I told you to stay out of my way," she snapped, unable to keep the hurt twisting inside her out of her voice. The wind had died down and the snow had diminished to nothing more than a flake or two swirling through the air from time to time. Snyder had radioed her with the word that the Chinook was in the process of hauling Walt's people to safety. All she wanted to do was get this rescue over with and go home.

She didn't want to think anymore.

Heath unzipped his parka with a jerk. His goggles dangled around his neck, as did hers and Littles's. "Just let me do this, Jayne. It's not a big deal."

He seemed damned steady for someone who'd almost freaked out on her during their last climb. "Not unless you panic," she retorted. Around this bend and over this little ridge would be a straight drop. Their rescue was most likely on that ledge. Maybe Heath hadn't figured that out yet, but she knew this terrain like the back of her hand.

"I've got it under control," he growled.

"Right," she quipped, smirking.

If he hadn't grabbed her by the arm she might have believed him. He'd spoken with fierce confidence. But she felt the tremble in his hands before his fingers tightened solidly around her.

Their gazes collided but he blinked away any fear before she could make it out.

"I'll lead," Littles butted in. "I'm the one with the badge and the weapon."

Jayne swore softly.

"What did he mean by that?" Heath demanded as the deputy moved past them.

She hadn't wanted to go into this with Heath. She knew he'd make something of it. "The sheriff had a bad feeling about this call." That's all she intended to say. She yanked her arm free of his grip. "Stop wasting my time."

Heath insisted on staying in front of her, but didn't slow her progress. "Tell me exactly what he said."

Jayne ignored him. If this man was injured—if it was Thurman McGill—she didn't want to waste any more time talking.

"Jayne, tell me—"

Heath froze.

It wasn't a particular sound or movement that stopped him in his tracks, rather it was the total lack of either.

Nothing.

The sound of the deputy's plunge through the fresh snow had been silenced. Nothing moved. If the deputy had encountered the victim, why didn't he say anything? Heath drew his weapon.

"Dammit!"

Jayne scrambled over the rock outcropping before Heath could grab her. She'd apparently sensed the same thing he had. He resisted the urge to call out to her. They rounded the slight dip and bend in the ridge at the same time.

Jayne abruptly stalled. "Dad?"

The word echoed in the air at the same time Heath's gaze landed on the man. He stood on the ledge as if he'd been dropped on that particular spot to wait for them. Deputy Littles lay at his feet.

Jayne would have rushed to aid her friend if Heath hadn't held her back.

Howard Stephens lifted one booted foot and pushed the deputy's too-still body over the edge. Jayne screamed, tried to tear away from Heath's hold.

"Don't move!" Heath commanded.

Stephens looked at him and laughed. "You must be kidding."

"Don't make me do this," Heath warned. Somewhere

deep inside him he'd known all along that it would come to this. Danes had put him in this position. Had ordered the man's execution.

Stephens shook his head. "Do you really think I'm worried about you shooting me in front of my own daughter? No. I don't think so. I know what the two of you have been up to."

"Don't you do this, Heath," Jayne cried. "Don't." Devastation echoed in her voice, she shook violently.

Heath couldn't look at her, had to keep his full attention on Stephens. But he didn't have to look. He knew that her eyes would be wide with terror, bright with emotion. And this son of a bitch didn't care.

"Come to me, Jayne."

"No way." Heath tightened his grip on her arm. "She's not coming near you."

"It's over now, Murphy," Stephens said. "I already have the answer I wanted. It's Cole Danes. But don't worry, he won't get away with this. Sending you here did nothing but sign his own death warrant."

Heath kept his expression carefully schooled. "This is over, Stephens. Throw down your weapon."

Stephens snorted. "Oh, that's right. You're not going to give away anything, are you? It's all about the assignment, right? You don't want to screw this up like you have everything else in your life."

Heath clenched his jaw hard to fight the impact of the words…the truth. He fought fire with fire. "Why don't you tell your daughter how you screwed up her life? Maybe tell her about what you helped do to the

Colby family or maybe show her your most recent kill list. I'm sure she'd find the names interesting reading."

Stephens took a bead right between Heath's eyes. "She'll never believe you over me. I'm still her father."

"You…you killed Deputy Littles," Jayne said, as if the realization had only just then penetrated.

"Come to me, Jayne," Stephens ordered. "I have a helicopter standing by. Let me take you away from this man. He only used you. He doesn't care about you."

Helicopter?

Jayne stared at her father. He stood on that ledge dressed much as she was, in full climbing gear. At first, she'd been confused. Lebron Littles was dead. Her father had pushed his body off the ledge. She squeezed her eyes shut, trying to blot out the image of him falling that bloomed in her mind's eye.

Her father had killed him. She hadn't heard the gunshot. Hadn't seen him do it, but it was true. Her mind just didn't want to accept it. Deputy Littles wouldn't have attempted to harm her father. There was no reason he would have represented a threat to her father…

Helicopter. Thurman McGill. Her father standing there with a gun. All the fragments coalesced in that instant.

"Did you hurt Mr. McGill? Did you use one of his helicopters to get up here and set this up?" Her eyes widened with her next thought. "It was you who called in the 9-1-1."

"Come to me now!" he commanded cruelly.

Jayne jerked at the sound. She hadn't heard her father shout like that since…memories flooded her. Long buried memories of a time when her father had done a lot of that. Shouting at her mother. Name calling. Cruel behavior. Her breath caught in a ragged gasp. How could she not have remembered?

"Drop your weapon, Stephens," Heath cautioned. "I don't want to have to shoot you, but I will."

"So shoot me," her father said, "and I'll shoot her. You think you can get a direct enough hit to stop me before I get one off? Trust me, Murphy, I won't miss."

Jayne went still. Heath felt the change.

"She's your daughter," Heath said, the words bitter on his tongue.

"I brought her into this world, I can take her out."

Jayne shuddered then abruptly wrenched away from Heath before he could stop her.

"Stay back, Jayne!"

She'd rushed straight up to her father before the warning stopped ringing in the air.

"Why are you doing this?" she asked as she peered up at the man she'd loved and made excuses for all these years. "I thought you loved me."

Heath readied his grip on his weapon at the sound of hurt in her voice. Killing this bastard was far too simple a fate for his heinous acts.

"I do love you," her father said, careful to keep his eye and his aim on Heath. "That's why I have to do this." He pulled Jayne close to his side, his full attention never leaving Heath. "You see, sweetheart, as long as you're alive they won't stop coming. Now that they know about us, they'll want to use you to get to me. I can't take that chance."

Heath snugged his finger around the trigger but couldn't risk the shot with her in her father's hold.

"Move away from him, Jayne," he urged, not completely successful at keeping the desperation out of his voice.

Jayne blinked, her brain still struggling with the harsh reality. The weapon in her father's hand twitched twice.

An almost inaudible hiss sliced the air after each twitch.

It took several seconds for Jayne to assimilate what her eyes saw. Heath fell to the ground. Her entire being went numb as her father released his hold on her long enough to kick Heath's weapon out of his reach.

She swayed but caught herself.

This couldn't be real.

She shook her head. Not real.

The hard clutch of her father's hands on her shoulders tore her from the dizziness of shock dragging at her consciousness.

"You understand why I have to do this, don't you, Jayne?"

Her gaze connected with his and for the first time in her life she did understand. He was her father. He loved her. But he was willing to sacrifice her or anyone else to save himself.

"Yes," she whispered, unable to push the words past her lips with anymore force than that. "I understand."

The wind whipped up a little, swirling snowflakes between them.

"Good." He released her. "Then I'll let you do the honors." He gestured to the precipice of the snow-covered ledge. "You're a good daughter, Jayne. I know you won't let me down."

He was right. Not once in her life had she ever let him down. She'd trusted him, believed in him despite all that he'd done to her mother…to her.

She thought of Heath lying there, unmoving on the ground. Was he dead? If not he would be soon. He'd come here to warn her…to protect her. She hadn't believed him, had been taught not to trust. She'd never been allowed to have anyone, not really…because of her father. She went very still inside as the haze of years of lying to herself cleared.

"There's just one thing," she said, looking deeply into her father's eyes.

"Be quick," he suggested, certain of his destiny. "My enemies are too close for comfort."

"You go first!" Jayne plowed into him with all her weight…with all the rage bursting inside her.

He went down, the lower part of his body dangling over the edge. She stumbled back, fear pounding in her chest. He clawed at the ledge, grabbed onto her leg. She hit the ground—tried to reach the weapon he'd dropped. He pulled her farther away…she couldn't reach it!

"You little bitch!" he screamed.

She felt herself sliding, moving over the ledge.

Jayne grappled for a handhold. Couldn't grab on.

Her hips followed her legs over the precipice.

She screamed. Tried to kick him loose.

He hung on.

The sound of a gunshot shattered the frigid air.

The weight dragging her downward fell free.

The sudden shift loosened her grip on the snowy ledge.

She cried out.

A hand clutched her forearm.

Halted her fall with a jerk.

Dangling in thin air, Jayne stared upward.

Heath's grip on her left arm was all that kept her from following her father's descent.

Her heart thundered in her throat, the ache of it swelling against her brain. If his grasp slipped… "God, don't let me fall."

Heath lay on his stomach flat against the ledge. He strained to grab on to Jayne with his left hand. If he could just get a hold of her with both hands he could pull her up.

"Please, Heath," she begged, "pull me up."

The panic hit him like a runaway train. Slammed into his gut. Paralyzed him. He'd been here before. His grip the only thing standing between the woman he loved and certain death.

The understanding in Jayne's eyes told him she knew what was happening. That he was helpless.

"You can do this, Heath. I know you can."

She swung her right hand up and snagged a handful of his parka sleeve.

Sweat beaded on his forehead. He couldn't move. If he moved a single muscle she would fall…he was certain, he'd done this before. He'd reached with his other hand and *she* had fallen.

A rush of weakness swept over him and he shuddered. Stephens had hit him in the side and in the thigh. He'd lost a lot of blood, wouldn't be able to hold out long. He couldn't save her.

"Reach for me, Heath," Jayne urged. "Reach with your left hand, too. Pull me up."

"You'll fall." Nausea churned in his gut.

"I trust you, Heath," Jayne whispered. "I know you can do this."

She hadn't listened…wouldn't reach up to him when he'd begged her to. That's why she'd fallen. God…that's why he hadn't been able to save her. Heath clenched his teeth hard, pushed past the fear and memories, reached toward Jayne with his left arm. His right arm trembled with the strain. He fastened onto her with both hands and pulled with all his might.

He howled with the pain and effort, his body trembling with the fatigue sucking at his ability to stay conscious. He didn't stop…didn't let go.

Suddenly she was up and over…falling onto the snow with him.

"Thank you." She gasped the words over and over.

He hugged her close, relief gushing through his veins. "If I'd lost you," he murmured against her cheek.

She drew back, touched his jaw. "You're not going to lose me."

"I'm sorry."

She shook her head. "You were right. I…" She let go a heavy breath, the ragged sound tearing at his heart. "I should have seen the truth before now."

Before he could respond, pain screamed through him on the heels of the receding adrenaline. "You're going…to—to be okay." He closed his eyes against the burn in his side. His leg had already gone numb.

She scrambled up and grabbed the radio clipped to her parka.

Heath closed his eyes and struggled to relax…to ignore the pain. In the background he heard her telling Snyder to send the Chinook but the sound kept fading and then coming back. He didn't want to pass out. She might need him. Stephens hadn't gotten here by himself. His buddies might show up.

"Heath." Jayne moved down next to him. He tried to open his eyes but couldn't manage. "Heath, help is on the way. I'm going to try and stop the bleeding. Stay with me, okay?"

He moved his lips but wasn't sure he actually spoke.

"Stay with me, Heath."

She sounded far away…in a tunnel or a cave.

"Heath…"

Chapter Sixteen

Heath gasped.

He opened his eyes. The room tilted, went blurry, then came back into focus.

White walls.

He moved his head slightly to the left—IV pole and bag.

Hospital.

Then Heath remembered. He had been shot. Stephens was dead.

"Jayne." His voice sounded rusty. His mouth and lips felt dry. He licked his lips and tried to sit up. A stab of pain sliced through him, forcing him back down. He groaned, his senses becoming suddenly aware of intense pain radiating through his entire body.

"You're out of surgery and stable, Murphy."

He opened his eyes to find Cole Danes standing over him.

"Where's Jayne?" He licked his lips again.

"She's just outside the door. I have a few questions and then you can see her."

"Stephens is dead. What else do you want?" If Heath hadn't been in such extreme pain he would have climbed out of the bed and beat the hell out of the guy.

"Correct. His body was identified one hour ago. The Chinook from Fort Carson that brought you and Miss Stephens off that mountain encountered a civilian helicopter en route to your position. I'm assuming the two men inside were Stephens's cohorts."

Heath bit back a groan. He'd be damned if he'd let Danes see his agony. "That's probably right. He mentioned something about them picking him up. We think he stole a helicopter from a local."

"Yes, a Thurman McGill. The sheriff found his body shortly after you arrived at the hospital."

"I want to see Jayne now," Heath insisted, uncertain how long he could handle this level of pain without passing out. He balled his hands into fists and struggled with the urge to just let go and pass out. Damn. Was it supposed to be like this?

"I need to know exactly what Stephens said to you," Danes instructed. "Don't leave anything out."

A realization somehow skirted its way through the fog of pain. Heath focused his weary gaze on Danes. "I was right. Something about this was personal between you and Stephens."

"Answer the question, Murphy." Danes's intent expression never wavered. He had his agenda and nothing was going to stop him. "I know you're in pain. Don't waste energy pretending otherwise."

A hiss of pain slipped past Heath's tightly clenched

teeth. "He knew it was you," he growled. "He…" Heath clenched his teeth again as a new wave of pain crashed through him.

"Tell me the rest, Murphy," Danes urged.

"He…" Heath swallowed as best he could. "He said you'd signed your own death warrant. That you wouldn't get away with it."

"Thank you, Murphy. You did well."

Heath clutched the bed rail with his free hand and lifted his head, defying the pain. "You risked too much, Danes," he accused. "Jayne could have been killed. How could you take that kind of chance?"

Danes paused at the door and looked back at him. "It was the only way."

He walked out without further explanation.

Heath collapsed, gasping to get air into his lungs.

When he got out of here he intended to tell Victoria just exactly what kind of man the Colby Agency had hired to conduct this internal affairs investigation.

If anyone could get this situation back under control, Victoria could.

"Heath?"

He knew an instant's relief at the sound of Jayne's voice. She rushed to his side and took his hand in hers.

"He wouldn't let me see you." Her eyes were red from crying.

For him, Heath thought, then he remembered she'd just lost her father.

"I'm sorry it had to happen this way, Jayne." She would hate him when the excitement had faded. When she'd had time to think. She would never want to see him again.

She squeezed his hand. "Let's not talk about that right now." She stared down at their hands a moment. "I'm still torn about my...about him." Her gaze settled back on Heath's. "I have to come to terms with that. It'll take time, I know." She smiled, but as sweet as it was, Heath saw the sadness just beneath the surface. "Right now all I'm worried about is you." She blinked uncertainly. "And us."

He rubbed his thumb over the back of her hand, ignoring the pain vying for his attention once more. "We're good," he assured her. There was so much more he could tell her that might help her get over her father faster. Like the fact that he'd killed at least one other man she'd cared about in the past, but what would be the point? She'd heard and seen more than enough. He wouldn't add anything else.

She shrugged, then swiped at her eyes. "I'm not sure I could ever leave this place."

He reached up, gritting his teeth against the pain knifing through his side, down his leg, and touched her cheek. "You don't have to worry about that. I don't think I'm cut out for investigative work anymore. Maybe Walt can use another guide."

The hope that sprang to life in her eyes almost undid him completely. "You're sure you're up for this kind of life? I know being here has been especially hard on you. I know about what happened on the Moses Tower."

That was a part of Heath's past that he would never forget, but the past few days had taught him that he couldn't go back. Couldn't change anything. He was only human, had made a terrible mistake. He had to try and move past it. The past belonged exactly there, in the past.

"I'll work it out." He cupped her soft cheek. "We both will. Time is all we need."

She bent down and brushed her lips against his, giving him another moment's reprieve from the agony. "I care very much for you, Heath." She swept the hair back from his forehead. "I think I might be in love with you." Her lips trembled.

He smiled, his heart brimming with emotion. Thank God he wasn't in this alone. "Remember, I said you weren't going anywhere without me?"

"I remember."

"That's a promise I intend to keep."

COLE DANES STOPPED at the nurses' station a few steps from Murphy's room. The head nurse glared at him as she rose from her chair like a warrior ready to do battle. Though they'd clashed once already, she still took the time to take in the length of his hair and the earring with a blatant look of distaste.

"I assume I can administer Mr. Murphy's pain meds now," she snapped, her expression furious, her voice scathing.

"You may."

She pivoted on her heel and hurried to do her duty. He respected vigilance even when it was at odds with his own.

Cole turned to the elevators directly across the corridor and depressed the call button. There was no point in explaining to the good nurse that he'd needed Murphy alert to answer his questions. Had he had his way he would have questioned him before surgery but Jayne Stephens had won that battle.

Only because Cole had allowed it, however. Even he wasn't without a respectable amount of compassion.

The cell phone in his jacket pocket vibrated. He moved slightly away from the area of the nurses' station as he took the call. "Danes."

"I want an update on Heath," Victoria Colby-Camp demanded with as much decorum as one could expect after all she'd heard this Sunday morning.

"His condition is stable," Cole told her without bothering with small talk since she hadn't. Small talk, polite conversation, that wasn't his style in any event. "The surgeon expects a full recovery."

"Thank God." The enormous relief she felt echoed across the line as clearly as her words.

A beat of weighty silence filled the air.

"What happens now, Mr. Danes?"

Her question was just shy of curt. Cole smiled. She didn't like him. Understandable.

"Now I return to Chicago to finish this."

"You're certain you've made no mistake."

The hesitancy in her tone was no surprise.

"Ask Lucas. He'll tell you. I never make mistakes." He moved back to the elevator as the doors glided open. "Trust me, *Victoria*, this investigation will be over soon and you will know why your most trusted employee betrayed you."

Cole dropped the cell back into his pocket and depressed the button for the lobby.

That was the thing about his line of work, he simply couldn't make it clear that there were no happy endings, only solved cases.

When he was finished there would be no more unanswered questions.

There would only be truth.

* * * * *

Coming next month, the shocking conclusion to
COLBY AGENCY INTERNAL AFFAIRS
PRIORITY: FULL EXPOSURE

like a phantom in the night
comes an exciting promotion from

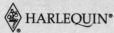

HARLEQUIN®

INTRIGUE®

ECLIPSE

GOTHIC ROMANCE

Look for a provocative
gothic-themed thriller each month
by your favorite Intrigue authors!
Once you surrender to the classic
blend of chilling suspense and
electrifying romance in these
gripping page-turners, there will
be no turning back....

Available wherever Harlequin books are sold.

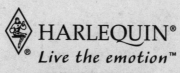

HARLEQUIN®
Live the emotion™

www.eHarlequin.com

HIE3

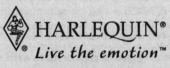

If you enjoyed what you just read,
then we've got an offer you can't resist!

Take 2 bestselling love stories FREE!

Plus get a FREE surprise gift!

Clip this page and mail it to Harlequin Reader Service®

IN U.S.A.	IN CANADA
3010 Walden Ave.	P.O. Box 609
P.O. Box 1867	Fort Erie, Ontario
Buffalo, N.Y. 14240-1867	L2A 5X3

YES! Please send me 2 free Harlequin Intrigue® novels and my free surprise gift. After receiving them, if I don't wish to receive anymore, I can return the shipping statement marked cancel. If I don't cancel, I will receive 4 brand-new novels each month, before they're available in stores! In the U.S.A., bill me at the bargain price of $4.24 plus 25¢ shipping and handling per book and applicable sales tax, if any*. In Canada, bill me at the bargain price of $4.99 plus 25¢ shipping and handling per book and applicable taxes**. That's the complete price and a savings of at least 10% off the cover prices—what a great deal! I understand that accepting the 2 free books and gift places me under no obligation ever to buy any books. I can always return a shipment and cancel at any time. Even if I never buy another book from Harlequin, the 2 free books and gift are mine to keep forever.

181 HDN DZ7N
381 HDN DZ7P

Name	(PLEASE PRINT)	
Address	Apt.#	
City	State/Prov.	Zip/Postal Code

Not valid to current Harlequin Intrigue® subscribers.

Want to try two free books from another series?
Call 1-800-873-8635 or visit www.morefreebooks.com.

* Terms and prices subject to change without notice. Sales tax applicable in N.Y.
** Canadian residents will be charged applicable provincial taxes and GST.
  All orders subject to approval. Offer limited to one per household.
® are registered trademarks owned and used by the trademark owner or its licensee.

INT04R   ©2004 Harlequin Enterprises Limited

eHARLEQUIN.com

The Ultimate Destination for Women's Fiction

Becoming an eHarlequin.com member is easy, fun and **FREE!** Join today to enjoy great benefits:

- **Super savings** on all our books, including members-only discounts and offers!

- Enjoy **exclusive online reads**—FREE!

- Info, tips and **expert advice** on writing your own romance novel.

- FREE romance **newsletters,** customized by you!

- Find out the latest on your **favorite authors.**

- Enter to win exciting **contests and promotions!**

- Chat with other members in our **community message boards!**

To become a member,
visit www.eHarlequin.com today!